Forgiveness
That Brought Me Love

Forgiveness
That Brought Me Love

written by:
Melissa J. Mallory

Mallory Media Enterprise LLC
2013

Dedication

To the author and perfecter of my faith, Jesus Christ, thank you for entrusting me with such a gift. I seek to make you proud.

To every person who has struggled with forgiveness and love won, great is your reward in heaven for you overcame and allowed love to reign in your hearts.

Matthew 26:28 (NKJV) - For this is My blood of the new covenant, which is shed for many for the remission of sins.

Acknowledgements

To one of my biggest cheerleader and greatest supporter, my love Stephen. Thank you for supporting my dream and making it a part of yours. Your desire to finally have my writing out for the world to see is what pushed me every day to continue. I love you and thank you from the bottom, top, and all sides of my heart.

To my parents, sisters, brothers, aunts, uncles, and cousins, thank you for being the best set of family members a girl could ask for. All the years we've had together has helped develop me into who I am. I love you guys.

chapter 1

Joyce Nickerson, what has gotten into you?

At the age of twenty-nine, she still wondered how she got herself in this situation. Her five feet, four inch medium frame was thrown across her couch, chocolate brown legs tangled around her throw pillows, and her cordless phone loosely dangled from her right hand to her right ear. She ran her hand through her black-blue dyed, newly cut spiky hair-do and looked at her freshly polished toes.

"Clint, all these years I thought I was saving myself for you," she grinned, shamelessly flirting with her close friend of seven years.

"Yeah, right. I see you take me for an idiot." Clint laughed, not picking up on Joyce's breathless giggle.

For the few years she'd known Clint, she had always been able to control her fantasies about him. She met him one night during her graduate year at the University of Miami in the school library. Nervously sitting at a table trying to figure out how she was going to complete her thesis within the next eight months, a pair of auburn arms came into view, and she prayed whoever it was would not interrupt. *When have my prayers ever been answered*, she'd thought to herself.

"Do you mind if I sit here with you? Looks like all the other tables are occupied."

She looked up to tell the baritone voice young man that this one was as well, when a pair of hazel eyes and pearly white teeth, with a gap in between, came into view. He stood close to six feet tall, his T-shirt clung to his perfectly shaped torso, and his bald-shaved head glistened in the light as if he just ran a marathon. She remembered telling herself, '*If God was black, this is what He would look like... the epitome of perfection*'. Her original rejection quickly melted away, and all she could do was smile in return and nod her head. Ever since that day, she had the biggest crush on Clint McCord, but wouldn't dare let him know that. She even went as far as encouraging him to date her childhood friend, I'neta. For seven years, she hadn't revealed how she truly felt; excluding that one crazy night... the night she was desperately trying to forget.

She switched the phone from one ear to the other, ignoring the nervous flutter in her stomach. "Clint, I seriously do not need a man to make or keep me happy, nor am I interested in being set up."

"It's not good for people to be alone, and having a man in your life can make you happy." Clint said, sounding more and more impatient. "You need to get out that house, Joyce. With all these eligible men running around Miami, there's no reason for you to be single."

"First of all, I'm not alone. And secondly, I do get out." Joyce let out an exasperated sigh, then kicked the throw pillow on the floor.

"Yeah, but with who? I'neta? "

"She's my best friend, Clint, and must I remind you, your ex-girlfriend."

"And there's a reason why she's my ex-girlfriend." He took a deep breath. "Wait a minute. I have another call coming in."

She exhaled loudly and wondered how she ever let her feelings mature for Clint. Not once had he gave an inclination that he wanted her. He was always hinting that a saved man needs a saved woman. That, in itself, disqualified her from any relationship they may have tried to pursue. Of course she goes to church— she just hadn't been in eleven years. Clint is an ol' saved-sanctified-filled with the Holy Ghost-fire baptized type of saint. That was the kind of woman he needed. That was the type of woman she was not. Clint needed someone who is outspoken and fearless. Joyce considered herself to be restrained and apprehensive. He needed an assertive, take action type of woman. Joyce felt she was too fragile to argue with anyone.

She did remember that one crazy night though. That night that changed her whole life, and could have changed their friendship. She ended up at Clint's place, crying and drooling all over his shirt, and not once did he complain. He held her until she fell asleep, whispering, *"it'll be alright. You need someone that's going to love you with a genuine love"*. She should have known he was talking about God. *Why did I make a fool out of myself?* The one time she tried to step up and take action, it backfired on her. Remembering his reaction after she tried to kiss him brought that feeling of shame and rejection back. She tried shaking the memories from her head as she waited for him to come back on the line.

Clint's baritone voice interrupted her thoughts. "Joyce, that's Eileen on the other end. We will have to finish this conversation later, but think about what I said. Edmund is a cool guy and I think you guys could hit it off."

"No need. I've already made up my mind." Knowing Clint was ready to interject, she abruptly ended the conversation. "Don't be rude by making your girlfriend wait for you on the other end. Tell her I said hello."

"I'll let this go for now. See you tomorrow for lunch."

"Goodbye, Clint."

She hung up with him and started to do what she did best when her thoughts were running rampant— clean. She loaded the dishes from last night's dinner into the dish washer, wiped every appliance in her kitchen, and scrubbed both of her bathroom showers. On her way to a mess of a bedroom, her phone rang and it took her a minute to find it under a pile of clothes.

Taking a deep breath she flopped herself on her bed. "Hello."

"Hey, you! You sound out of breath. What were you doing?" I'neta asked.

"Only you would call someone you haven't spoken to in two weeks and demand answers. Where have you been?" Joyce asked, somewhat irritated.

"Girl, it's a long story. How about I tell you over lunch? Say... three-ish?"

"Lunch would be nice. I need to get out of this house." Joyce rolled over unto her stomach and allowed her legs to dangle at the foot of her bed. "You won't believe how tired I am."

Laughing out loud, I'neta said, "Tired? From what I've heard, you haven't been doing anything but sitting in your house for the last couple of weeks."

"And how would you know that?"

"Your secretary, Ms. Ruby. You know she worries about you like a mother hen. And from the little she's told me today, you're supposed to be resting, not out of breath. What *were* you doing? Am I interrupting anything? Do you have... company?"

"Woman, please! If I had anyone here taking my breath away, I truly would not be answering this phone. I was cleaning."

"Cleaning? On a Friday morning? Hmm. You must have a lot on your mind. Yeah, let's do lunch. Does Monty's Exquisite sound good?"

"Yeah, it does actually." Joyce sighed. "Maybe we can do a little shopping downtown at the boutiques. Now that spring is here, they'll have a few winter items on sale."

"You know I love any excuse to shop, but I can't today. I have a counseling session with a client of mine," I'neta replied.

"OK. I'm almost done cleaning. I'll see you in a bit. Love ya."

"Ditto."

She hung up and placed the phone back on the receiver. *That I'neta,* she thought to herself.

When she met I'neta Villanucci, it was hate at first sight. Every day in first grade they would taunt each other until someone pulled them apart. When they realized that neither one was willing to give in, they decided to join forces and bully the other children. *How could two six year olds take on the whole first grade class,* Joyce pondered. *We were a force to be reckoned with.*

An hour later, Joyce showered, pulled on a pair of black jeans, slipped on an old university T-shirt, and tied some old black running shoes on her feet. She stared at herself in the mirror, then shrugged. *This will just have to do.* By the time she pulled up to the restaurant, I'neta was getting out of her car. She looked her over and wondered how they ever became friends.

I'neta owned a pair of long legs, which seemed like they went on forever. The blue calf-length skirt she wore did her legs much justice and her curves no room to breathe. The white blouse, buttoned half way up, showed off just enough cleavage to be modest. Joyce never understood why I'neta still chose to wear six inch heels, as she gazed down at the blue pumps I'neta sported. She thought to herself, as she always did when she sees her best friend, *How and why did God put us together? We're so different, I even wonder how we get along. She's gorgeous and I'm... well... I'm just me.*

I'neta wasn't the all-American type of beauty, but her dazzling features drew in looks. Her Trinidadian and Italian heritage contributed to her high cheekbones, lengthy hair that flowed down her back, and tan complexion. She had a slight dimple that showed on her left cheek when she laughed. Where Joyce thought she was restrained, apprehensive, and fragile, I'neta was assertive, outspoken, and fearless. Her 'get-it-all-or-lose-it-all' attitude was what Joyce admired most about her dear friend. *What else can a man ask for? While I'neta gets all the stares, I get all the leftovers,* she thought.

I guess God was asleep when He made me, Joyce thought as she stepped out her car. *On the seventh day God rested, and haphazardly made me.* She smirked at her own cruel joke as she made her way to I'neta.

Waiting for her at the entrance of the restaurant, I'neta said, "Hey, Gorgeous." She eyed Joyce up and down. "What is wrong with you?"

Joyce looked down at herself. "What?"

"What?! T-shirt and jeans? You've never come out in public looking like that. We have to talk."

She grabbed Joyce's hand and pulled her inside the restaurant. Joyce dragged herself along and wondered what was up with I'neta. I'neta always worried about how others saw her, but she also knew Joyce could care less about that. *Guess she's embarrassed with being seen with me in public like this, huh,* she thought to herself. She sat across from I'neta and ran her hand through her hair. *Ever since my hair cut, this running my hand through my hair business has been a bad habit.*

A waiter came over to take their orders and couldn't take his eyes off I'neta's cleavage. *Well... if I was in his shoes, I probably wouldn't either*, Joyce thought. He finished taking their orders and poured them a glass of water each without even giving Joyce a glance. She rolled her eyes and folded her own napkin on her lap before he could do it for her.

I'neta gave him a flirtatious smile, then rolled her eyes when he turned away. Turning to give Joyce her full attention, she said, "Men are ridiculous. Well... how long are we going to sit here before you tell me what's wrong, Joyce?"

"I don't know where to start," Joyce said, staring into her glass.

"What do you mean you don't know where to start? And why do I have to find out from your secretary that you've been out for two weeks?"

Taking a sip of her water, Joyce swallowed the frustration building up. "I've tried calling you a couple of times, I'neta. Once, some dude answered and said you couldn't come to the phone," Joyce said, giving her a suspicious look.

I'neta blushed and looked away. "Oh, well... I'll explain that later."

"That or him?" asked Joyce, knowing the twinkle in her friend's eyes meant this man was more than a friend.

"Both," I'neta murmured. Clearing her throat, she quickly changed the topic. "Now, tell me what's been going on with you."

Joyce sighed loudly, knowing what her friend was doing. "Two weeks ago, I got into a car accident."

"A car accident! Oh my God, J. Are you alright?" She looked closely at Joyce's face for any scars that may have appeared within the last few seconds.

"I'm sitting here, aren't I? It wasn't that serious on my end. Just a few cuts and bruises on my arms and chest, but the other woman," she looked away, "she didn't make it. Technically, it wasn't my fault, but I still felt like there was something I could have done while we waited for the ambulance. All I did was held her hand. I couldn't even pray, given the fact that I haven't spoken to God in years."

Her voice caught as she replayed that night in her mind. She took a deep breath to steady herself. "She fell asleep behind the wheel and ended up swerving to my lane. At the hospital, I had the chance to meet her husband... a pastor." She took a sip of water avoiding I'neta's eyes. "He sat beside me the entire time. Consoling me and telling me that it wasn't my fault. All of a sudden we were talking about God..."

"And?" I'neta asked, with her entire body tensed. Joyce knew I'neta didn't like where this conversation was headed, but she couldn't help what had happened. She couldn't help the feeling of being lost.

Joyce shook her head. "I don't know. Lately... I've been thinking about my life and... it feels like something is missing." She finally looked I'neta in the eyes, "You know what I mean?"

"No. Don't get tied up in that religious mess, Joyce. Take it from me. You know what I've been through." I'neta's face turned sour. Joyce could tell she was fighting off the old ugly memories.

"I do... but, I can't help but think—"

"It's a waste of time. Those people are frauds. Only out to take advantage of you." I'neta took a sip of her water, realizing she was raising her voice. She exhaled and placed her cup down. "They only want to use you, Joyce. Take it from someone who knows personally."

So much bitterness was laced in her voice, Joyce always wondered where it all came from. *Did I miss something growing up?*

"Not all of them are like that. Look at Clint," Joyce argued.

"Devil in disguise. Just give him a while..."

"Clint has never done anything to make you think he wasn't sincere about his faith." Joyce said, defending her friend.

"That's because I didn't give him the time to. A few more months with me would have revealed how he truly is."

"You don't believe that as much as I do. Well... the pastor invited me to his church, and I've considered going." She took another sip of her water and stared at her napkin before saying, "Actually, I've already visited his church once, and I really enjoyed it."

I'neta stared at her in disbelief. "Why, Joyce? What is it that you want from a life like that? I've tried it..." She shook her head, unable to finish her sentence.

"Can you really tell me that you feel more fulfill now, I'neta? Do you not feel there's something missing," she pointed towards her own chest, "in here?"

"The only thing I have in my heart is bitterness towards those people for what they put me through." I'neta quickly spat out. "Love? No. Forgiveness? Yeah, right. Bitterness? Always. Why love those that profess to have The One who created love but show no signs of it?"

Those were questions Joyce couldn't answer right now, so she opted not to. "Enough of that. Tell me about this guy that's answering your phone." She had to quickly change the subject before their lunch became as sour as their moods.

It took I'neta a minute to calm herself down, but she finally did. She did a short version of the breathing exercise she taught in her 'Women As Gold' counseling sessions every night. When she finally got herself together, her beautiful cheekbones enlarged from the smile plastered on her face.

"Well," I'neta blushed, "I met him a few months ago—"

"A few months ago?! And I'm now finding out? That's fowl, I'neta." She rolled her eyes and feigned a hurt expression.

"I didn't want to say anything until I knew that this one was heading somewhere. After the breakup with Timothy, I felt like I kept jumping from man to man, and well," she briefly looked at Joyce before looking away. "I didn't want you thinking the same."

Joyce smiled. "Girl, please. You have your mistakes, as I do mine, but being a romantic is not one of them. It's natural to want a relationship."

"Well, Mason is... something else. He's very romantic and loving." She sighed softly, going into a daydream. "He just seems too good to be true. Everything is perfect right now, and well... you know my luck."

Joyce reached over to squeeze I'neta's hand. "That was one messed up relationship. We're allowed at least ten."

I'neta squeezed her hand in return and smiled. "Good theory, but not true. The one thing that scares me is that he seems a little on the aggressive side."

Joyce gasped loudly. "Has he hit you?" With the look that passed across I'neta's face, she wondered if she would tell her the truth.

She never took I'neta for the submissive, passive type when it came to a man raising his hand. She could remember the time when I'neta was sixteen and some neighborhood punk slapped her fourteen-year-old sister, Beatrice. One minute I'neta was outside talking, the next minute she had already ran inside the house, grabbed her mother's pistol, and had it aimed at the boy's head. With tears streaming down her face, all she kept on murmuring was, *No one hits my sister*. It took Joyce, Beatrice, and both of their mothers to coax the gun out of her hand. Ever since that day, no guy has ever come across her front porch.

"No. Not that kind of aggressive. More like... possessive. One night while we were in bed, he told me he didn't want me talking to any more of my male friends after a certain time of night," I'neta shared with a nervous laugh. "I laughed and told him I left both of my parents in New Jersey." She shrugged, "It's things like that, that gets me." She picked up her glass of water to hide a look that crossed her face.

"How long is a few months?" Joyce questioned, with irritation lacing her voice.

"Four, maybe five months."

"And you're already sleeping with the guy?"

"Yeah, girl. I know, I know." I'neta ran her hand over her face, but not quick enough to hide her blush.

"You're using protection, right?"

The look I'neta gave Joyce would have scared her if she didn't know her. "Of course, Joyce. After Timothy..." she smirked. "I'm not stupid, OK. I was then, but I'm not now. Give me the benefit of the doubt."

"I would, but never would I've thought you'd sleep with a man within a few months of knowing him."

"Give me a break, Joyce," she said, slamming her water glass on the table. "I didn't ask to see you to hear you fuss."

I'neta's anger sparked Joyce's. *All I'm trying to do is help her see*, Joyce angrily thought.

You have to first be able to see before you can help anyone else see, she heard a still voice say.

"What kind of friend would I be if I told you what you wanted to hear instead of what you needed to hear, I'neta? Do you want me to tell you that it's OK to sleep around with every guy that knocks on your door? Well, it's not." Joyce yelled that last comment, causing patrons from surrounding tables to turn and look in their direction.

I'neta stared at her without saying anything for a brief second. "Did you just call me a...?"

"No, I did not. I'm making a point, I'neta. It's not healthy or sane to be sleeping with some man you barely know. Its borderline crazy if you ask me—" Her comment was cut short by the scraping of I'neta's chair on the wooden floor.

I'neta grabbed her purse and stood up. "Well, I didn't ask you, and never do I remember stating your opinion mattered to me right now." She rolled her eyes and shook her head. "This is exactly why I didn't want to tell you. All I need right now is to be able to talk to my best friend without being judged. I hear enough of this crap from my mother, who really doesn't have any room to tell me anything."

Crap?! We're trying to help her and she calls it crap? Joyce thought as she stood to grab I'neta's hand. "Sit down, I'neta, and quit the drama. It's me and you know I didn't mean any harm by it. I'm just worried about you. Ever since Timothy…" waved her hand in the air. "We'll leave that alone. I just don't want you getting messed up like you did before."

"Just trust me, Joyce. We both made mistakes in the past. Look at your relationship with Noel. That didn't work out but you're not messin' up with other guys because of it," she pointed out, taking her seat.

Joyce sat down and ignored the sting from I'neta's comment. "That's because I'm not trying to date any guys."

"My point exactly. That's the difference between me and you. I'm not letting Timothy keep me from finding my true mate the way you're allowing Noel keep you from finding yours."

Joyce opened her mouth to comment but nothing came out. That was one thing she could honestly say she loved about her best friend. She said whatever was on her mind. Before she could say anything else, the waiter returned with their food and the subject was dropped.

chapter 2

THIS IS GETTING worse each time I see him. What is up with that, Joyce asked herself as she sat across the restaurant table from Clint, watching him eat his pasta. *I've never had to deal with my feelings for him this much over the last few years. Maybe it's because I haven't had a real date with a man in years. Maybe I'neta is right; maybe I'm allowing Noel to have control over my life even while he's in prison.*

Or maybe I'm preparing your heart to receive me.

Joyce spat out the tea she was sipping on just then. She stared at Clint with bulging eyes. "What did you just say?"

Clint looked at Joyce crazily, then swallowed what was in his mouth before answering. "What are you talking about? I didn't say anything."

"Are you sure? 'Cause I could have sworn I heard someone say something... very loud and clear."

Clint twirled another fork of pasta and gave her another crazy look before placing it in his mouth. With his mouth full, he said, "I didn't say anything. You must be losing your mind, but that's probably because you haven't been out with a man in God knows how long."

Joyce picked up a napkin and wiped her mouth. She cleared her throat and took a careful sip of her tea. "Here we go again."

"Yes, here we go again," Clint responded, twirling another fork of pasta. "So, tell me... have you decided if you would go on a date with my friend?" He knew Joyce was getting tired of his matchmaking, but he was worried she would allow her fears to keep her alone. The last time he saw her with a man was maybe three years ago, and she quickly ended it when things started going well.

"I made my decision yesterday," she answered, rolling her eyes. "Come on, Clint. I'm not ready for a relationship right now."

She started to pick at her cherry cheesecake, feeling a sudden loss of appetite. Avoiding his eyes and hoping not to get into this conversation with Clint, she said, "Plus, I don't think I'm up for the extra drama of adding another person to my small group of friends." She gave up on eating and placed her fork down. "And I don't think... no, scratch that. I know I'm not ready for marriage, and a man that age, I'm sure, is looking for a wife."

"Well... maybe he is, but I'm not asking you to marry the guy. A few dates don't turn into marriage all of a sudden. Just go out with him a few times and enjoy yourself for once with someone other than I'neta."

Joyce stared at Clint trying to read his expression, hoping she could see some sign of why he was really pushing for this date. "What is it to you? Why are you trying to push me on this guy? Is he crazy or something?"

"No, he is not crazy. I'm just worried about you." Clint picked up his fork and ate another forkful of pasta. "You're a beautiful woman and you're letting your past relationship with Noel keep you from having a nice friendship with a decent, God-fearing man... shoot, with any man, for that matter." He wiped his mouth with his napkin and gave her his full attention.

Feeling agitated, Joyce threw her hands in the air. "That's the second time I've heard that this week. I am not letting Noel do anything. He's done enough. My decision has nothing to do with him. I'm just... okay right now without a man."

"And that's because you're afraid to jump into another relationship. Only because some stupid fool couldn't distinguish the difference between his woman and a punching bag." Seeing the hurt look on her face, Clint softened his tone. "He was never worth your time, anyway. You need more healthy relationships, Joyce."

"I have I'neta... and I have you," Joyce said. Although she sometimes felt lonely when neither one of her friends could be reached, she was satisfied with just having the two of them in her life. Fewer friends equaled less drama. "And I have my mother." She forced herself to eat, although her stomach was doing summersaults.

"You know what I mean. You need someone that could possibly be more than just a friend in the future."

I guess that counts you out, huh.

"Shoot, with your line of business," Clint smiled mischievously, "I'm surprised you don't have a few men chasing you."

Joyce gave him a sassy look, "I don't mix business with pleasure. Plus, men are intimidated by women who have their own business. You all want someone who makes you feel needed."

"Who told you that? I am glad my woman has a job. That way she can pay her half of the bill when we go out. And don't let her turn around and start her own business; she'll be paying my bill too."

Joyce laughed, knowing her friend would never let a woman pay his way. "That's what you call a very cheap date."

"Call it what you want, but I'm training her now." He laughed, glad to see Joyce relax some.

Clint allowed the tension to ease before going back to the conversation. "But seriously, Joyce, give Edmund a try. He really is a great guy. He has his head on straight, and I think you both will hit it off great."

Joyce sighed, hoping Clint would just drop it. Staring at her half-eaten cheesecake, she asked, "Why not set him up with your sister?" *And leave me alone.*

Clint looked at her as if she just morphed into something disgusting. "Because, even though I love Renee, we both know she's not ready to have any kind of relationship."

"And I am?" she asked, sarcastically. "I'm nowhere near as ready as your sister is."

"J, you have so much to offer a man. You're logical, supportive, honest." He reached over to touch her hand. "You're a great cook, and a beautiful woman. Any man would be happy to have you."

She looked at his hands on top of hers and thought to herself, *if this man only knew, he would stop touching me like this. A woman could only take but so much.*

She avoided his eyes and stared at her plate. "If that's the case, why did you turn me away?" It took everything in her to let those words flow out of her mouth. Just the thought of how he turned away from her that night made her feel inadequate and insignificant again.

I knew that was coming, Clint thought to himself. He pulled his hand away after a brief squeeze and replied, "Because you didn't really want me, J. You were at a drastic point in your life. You'd just lost your child and had your fiancé thrown into prison. You needed something or someone to cling to, and I just happened to be right there."

Oh, so that's what that was? Thanks for telling me how I truly felt.

She groaned her frustration loudly. "Fine. When do I get to meet this Edmund?" She quickly changed the subject.

Clint looked as if he wanted to finish the conversation they just started. He didn't like things brewing over his head, and what happened a few years ago between them had been brewing long enough. He changed his mind once he saw the look on Joyce's face. Shame, fear, and something else he couldn't put his hands on.

"You'll get to meet him this coming weekend. I'm having a dinner party at my house."

"Hmm. Who's cooking?" Joyce asked him suspiciously. "Everyone who has taste buds knows you can't."

He smiled and winked at her. "That's where you come in. What better impression to leave on a guy than your favorite casserole dish."

"You mean your favorite casserole dish, and I'm not cooking it. I'm the invited one, remember."

"You are. But before you disagree, I just need you to make that one dish. Renee and Eileen are making the rest."

"All right, I'll do it, but only if I'neta gets to come to dinner," she lifted her hand and quiet his response. "I need her to be the buffer just in case I'm not feeling this dude. You'll be too busy entertaining guests."

Clint hesitantly agreed. "OK, but you should know I wouldn't set you up with someone as half crazy as you are."

"Good." She looked at her watch. "Looks like our time is up. I have to meet I'neta at six." She stood up and gave him a kiss on the cheek. "Thanks for lunch. Next time, my treat." She grabbed her Coach purse, pushed her chair in, and started walking away.

"Next time we're going to La Chez de Souphant and I'm ordering the most expensive thing on the list." He mumbled to himself, "Leave me with a bill of forty-six dollars and it's just the two of us." He raised his voice so she could hear. "Girl, you know you can eat."

She waved her hand without looking back, and with a laugh on her lips said, "Love you, Sweetie. You're a Godsend."

She walked away, oblivious of all the stares she was getting. Clint also looked at her and couldn't help but smile. *For a short woman, she sho' is feisty. I don't know what I would do without that girl.* He remembered in the beginning of their friendship how she would question him about the girls he dated, and what he stood for as a Christian. Knowing she was watching how he lived made him make up his mind to live right. He gave up the pretense of not knowing better, especially since his mother was an evangelist and his father was a minister. He assumed when he came to college, he would take a break from church, but no matter how hard he tried what he was taught as a child was always there to remind him who he was.

God, if she would just see who she really is.
In due time.
"Thank you, God."

❊ ❊ ❊

Nearly emptying out her closet, Joyce tried on every outfit she placed her fingers on. She was now draped in a black dress that hid everything. The collar barely showed her neck, the sleeves covered her wrist bone, and the bottom draped all the way to her ankles. She glanced at herself in the mirror, then turned to look at I'neta. Lying backwards on the bed, with her feet propped up on the wall, she gave Joyce a funny look and shook her head.

"What's wrong with this one?" Joyce asked.

She knew it looked a little ridiculous, but this wasn't her wedding day. This was one date she was having with some man she really wasn't interested in, just to get Clint and I'neta off her back. Especially since Clint made it a point to introduce him to her last weekend at his dinner party.

Joyce was standing in the kitchen talking to Renee, when Clint walked in along with a medium built man he introduced as Edmund. Renee gave Clint a knowing smile then walked out of the kitchen. Clint lingered for some small chit chat before walking out with some excuse about checking on the chip bowls.

Joyce was not sure what else she and Edmund talked about, but by the end of the conversation she agreed to go on a date with him the following weekend. Not because she was interested in him, but because she knew Clint wouldn't stop matchmaking if she didn't, and she wanted to prove Noel was not controlling her social life.

As she got dressed for this date with Edmund, she purposely chose items that didn't compliment her shape. Not even sure where she got the dress from, she arched her eye brow at I'neta.

I'neta rolled her eyes at Joyce. "You look like a missionary on judgment day. Come on, now. It's not even fall yet. Plus... that dress doesn't throw the right signals. You want something that will captivate his mind and stay there for a long time."

"Do I need to remind you that he is a Christian man. I'm not trying to seduce the poor guy." She looked herself over and grimaced. *This really does look ridiculous, Sister Mary Clarence,* Joyce thought to herself.

"Girl, please. A man is a man. If you tempt them hard and long enough," I'neta responded, giving her a wink, "they'll fall."

"And that's exactly how you got into that mess with Timothy," Joyce carelessly said, regretting it as soon as it came out of her mouth.

I'neta's feet stopped the rhythmic pattern it was doing against the wall and everything in her screamed to retaliate to what Joyce just said. She slowly readjusted herself to sit upright on the bed and gave Joyce a blank stare. "Out of everyone, I never would have thought you felt that way about what happened." Hurt and disappointment flashed in her eyes for a second, before she concealed it. She refused to allow anyone to see her hurt. Not even her best friend. Not since Timothy did what he did to her.

Timothy Dallas was a minister at one of the popular churches almost every college student was attending, even I'neta. Timothy was tall-dark-and-handsome, single with no children and the pastor's armor bearer, which made him receive a lot of attention from women, with the exception of I'neta. She was attending the church for a year when he started to show her some interest. At the time, I'neta was a sophomore in college, trying to get her life straight, and decided that dating a minister would be much better than dating some of the men she had been introduced to. Little did she know Minister Dallas had a whole lot of skeletons in his closet.

It started off with him taking her out to dinner and to the movies. Then it moved on to personal Bible studies at her place. After a while, he started coming over all sorts of time at night, and sooner than later, he started spending nights. They began to get a little intimate, and then it went on to being something more serious. He started to talk about marriage and children, and making her the First Lady of the church when the pastor handed it over to him. I'neta knew everything they were doing was wrong, but she wasn't as strong as she thought. He claimed that he wanted them to get married soon, so that justified the fornication. A few months after they started dating, I'neta found out she was pregnant. Timothy tried to convince her to get an abortion, then left her when she refused to. Since then, she had sworn off ministers, church people, and church.

Looking at her friend now, Joyce wished she could take those words back. She took a hesitant step towards I'neta. "I'm sorry, I'neta. That came out the wrong way."

"Out of the heart the mouth speaks," I'neta replied, getting up off the bed. "Don't worry about it. That was years ago, and I know I didn't seduce him. That's all that matters." She reached under the bed to grab her shoes. "I'm going to grab a bite to eat. I'll be back in enough time to do your hair." She slipped on her shoes without looking at Joyce, and walked out the bedroom. "By the way, go with the choir robe you have on. It's less seductive." Joyce's front door sounded with a slam.

Joyce knew I'neta was passed the point of upset because she walked away. Walking away was a decision she made after a few crazy incidents like the one she had with the neighborhood boy and her sister. That was the only way to control herself.

God I didn't mean to say that, Joyce thought to herself.

She jumped in the shower hoping she would get the opportunity to really apologize to I'neta. She got out the shower and slipped on a button down cream dress that stopped a little above her knees. The collar dipped a little low, but not enough to show any cleavage. She slid on her navy blue pumps and accessorized her outfit with dangling navy blue earrings and a blue bracelet. By the time she was ready to comb her hair, I'neta walked into the house without saying a word and picked up the hot curler to stack up her curls. Twenty minutes passed without her saying a word to Joyce.

"I'neta," Joyce reached up to touch her arm.

"Don't talk to me, Joyce. I'm still angry with you. Let's just leave it alone for now, OK?"

Yep, she's upset, Joyce confirmed with herself, sighing real loud.

"Don't do that," I'neta's said, voice rising up a notch.

"Don't do what?"

"Huff and puff like I'm the one who's wrong. You've always done that. Since we were kids, and I've always found myself apologizing. Not this time."

"I was just wondering how I was going to fix this."

"Well, you can't right now."

I'neta finished combing her hair, then left without saying a word.

Joyce didn't want this to sour the mood tonight, so she sat down on her couch to keep herself from doing busy work, and decided to give herself a pep talk.

Take a deep breath and worry about apologizing to I'neta later. You're going out with a man who is good, funny, and smart. You are going to enjoy yourself, okay… even if it's just this one time.

Fifteen minutes later, Edmund showed up with a bouquet of red roses and a wide tooth grin. She smiled in return and took the flowers, hoping to forget how she hurt I'neta. She looked into his eyes but all she saw were the tears I'neta tried to hide when she walked out. Joyce shook her head and groaned, *this is going to be a long night.*

chapter 3

EDMUND DEVEREAU IS really a handsome man, Joyce thought to herself. He stood about six feet tall and weighed close to two hundred pounds. His dark complexion appeared to have been smeared with a rich chocolate candy bar, his hair neatly trimmed as well as the beard and mustache he sported, and his big brown eyes sat well on his face. He had deep dimples that were barely noticeable until he smiled. And every time he spoke his voice reminded her of water— smooth.

At the age of thirty-five, he seemed to have done well having his Masters in Biological Engineering, and being CEO of his grandfather's company. Best of all, he had an awesome sense of humor. From when she first took the flowers to the time he dropped her off at her home, she couldn't stop laughing, or maybe it was blushing. Whatever it was, it kept a smile on her face and I'neta off her mind. *I could do this. I could see myself enjoying his company*, Joyce thought.

He walked her to her door and waited for her to unlock it. He was as nervous as she was, and it showed by the dangling of the keys in both their hands. They both looked at each other and laughed before he cleared his throat and broke the silence.

Putting his hands in his pockets, he looked like he was back in the tenth grade trying to gain the courage to ask a girl out. "I had a good time tonight," Edmund said.

She smiled at his shyness. "So did I."

"Does that mean I get the privilege of taking you out again?"

"I would very much like that. Just give me a call and we can set something up." She took the risk of stepping closer and wrapping her arms around his waist to give him a hug, not sure how he would interpret it. The way he wrapped his arms around her and the slight air she felt on her neck when he exhaled felt too good. She stepped back and avoided his eyes hoping she wasn't too forward. "I'll also make sure to thank Clint for introducing us. I really did have a great time, Edmund."

Clearing his throat again, he looked at his watch and realized it was earlier than he thought. Knowing she wouldn't be comfortable inviting him in, and really hating to end the date, he started to pull at straws. "Umm... it's still kind of early. How about we take a ride around town and see what else we can get into without getting into trouble. Maybe coffee or something."

She looked at her watch and saw it was going on nine o'clock. *A ride around town wouldn't hurt.*

"Sure." She placed her keys back into her purse, and smiled at him. "Where did you have in mind?"

"Don't know. We can just ride with the flow."

He followed her back to his SUV and helped her get in. He jumped into the driver's side and sat there in silence for a while. "How do you feel about a stroll around Bayside?"

"That sounds great. I've always wanted to take a ride on one of those party boats."

"Well, tonight is your night." He looked at her and smiled at the excitement in her eyes.

The first thing Joyce noticed when they pulled up to Bayside were the lights that glared from inside the strip. They walked around looking at different craft booths and interesting items people were selling. They listened to a reggae band and entertained themselves watching those bold enough to dance. Edmund paid for them to take a short boat ride for an hour, which Joyce really enjoyed.

The view of the ocean from the deck was breathtaking. The street lights from above the bridge and the moon light danced in the reflection of the sea. The other passengers were up dancing and laughing, but it seemed like she and Edmund were in their own little world. He sat next to her, head tilted back, eyes closed, and lips parted ever so slightly as if he was softly asleep. She took that opportunity to admire his strong features. Without warning, he opened his eyes and stared directly into hers. Instead of blushing and cutting off the connection, she smiled and placed her hand on his.

"I've lived here for eleven years and never had a better time," Joyce said.

"Glad to know I'm the man who gave that to you."

Joyce tapped his hand playfully and chuckled. "Spoken like a true man. It's all about competition, huh?"

"No, it's all about making sure when you think of this night or come back to this place, you'll think of me."

"Like I said, spoken like a true man," she said, laughing out loud. "But, you are right. I don't think I'll think of Bayside without thinking of you. This has been one of the greatest dates I've had in a while." She squeezed his hand before letting go. "Thank you."

"The pleasure was all mine." He stood up, looking at his watch. "Now that the boat has stopped, I think it's time for us to be headed home. I would love to spend more time with you, but it's getting late and..."

She stood up and grabbed her purse. "And you're trying to be a gentleman. That's quite different from what I'm use to." She allowed him to hold her hand and walked her through the boat and down the stairs.

"Well, I apologize there aren't enough men like me who know how to treat women. But we're out there, Joyce." He stopped walking suddenly, and turned to look her directly in the eye. "And if you allow me the chance to keep that beautiful smile on your face and that sparkle in your eyes, I will show you how you deserve to be treated." He brushed his fingers across her cheek and looked like he was about to kiss her, but pulled himself together. Seeing the nervousness in her eyes, he smiled, "But that's if you can handle all this manliness."

She started walking still holding his hands, and giggled from the nervousness that crept its way up her spine. "Said like that, Mr. Devereau, you may get that chance not knowing what you're getting yourself into."

"That's a risk I'm willing to take, Joyce."

If you only knew. She smiled at him, again, as they walked back to his SUV in silence.

He's really a charming man, but please God, don't let this be another Noel.

She's beautiful, Father, but if she's another Gloria... please order my steps.

They allowed the soft sound of jazz to fill the car with noise instead of conversation. He reached her house and helped her out of the car.

"This was a beautiful evening," Edmund said, unlocking her door for her. "Hopefully, this will not be our last."

"I can guarantee that. You have a goodnight's sleep, Edmund. I'll speak with you tomorrow."

"Goodnight. Now, get inside so I can get going."

She gave him a hug and left him on her front porch counting the hours he would see that beautiful smile again.

❋ ❋ ❋

By the time Joyce pulled off her dress, pulled on an extra large t-shirt, and got comfortable in bed, I'neta was back on her mind. She looked at the clock and saw that it was one thirty in the morning. *Well, she'll be up*, thought Joyce. Positioning herself so that she was leaning against her head board, she picked up the phone and dialed I'neta's number.

"Took you long enough," I'neta answered on the first ring. "I take it your date went well?"

"Yes, it went very well." Joyce paused for a few seconds before apologizing. "I'm so sorry, I'neta. I—"

I'neta interrupted her, "I just can't believe you would say something like that to me after you know what I've been through with that jerk. It made me wonder if you thought that all along."

"No, Net. I know you better than that. I didn't mean it the way it sounded. I really am sorry."

"Sorry or not, it still hurt, J." I'neta said.

"I'm sorry, Love. I didn't mean it."

Heaving a sigh, I'neta changed the subject. "So... how was your date?"

She turned the lamp off and slid down underneath her blanket. "I'neta, I had so much fun tonight, it doesn't make any sense. He's nothing like I had in mind, you know... the all saved-sanctified type," Joyce said breathlessly. "Not saying that he tried anything. On the contrary, he was the most perfect gentleman I've ever met. You wanna know something, I'neta?"

"What, Girl?"

"A chick can actually have fun on a date without getting physical with a guy. Not even a kiss. That was a first for me, and..." Joyce couldn't put into words what she felt.

"So, I take it you're seeing this guy again," I'neta asked.

"Well, don't sound too happy for me," she said, sarcastically.

"I am happy for you. Happy that you've finally let someone take you out. I'm just real tired, J. So, we'll have to finish this conversation tomorrow."

"Are you OK?" Joyce was so tied up on her feelings, she nearly missed the depressing tone in her friend's voice.

I'neta took a while to answer. "I will be. I've had a long day and an even longer week. My body's just shutting down. I'll be OK. See you tomorrow?"

"I guess so. Same place?"

"Same time."

"Love you."

"Ditto," I'neta responded. She hung up without saying goodbye or goodnight, but that's how I'neta was.

Joyce hoped one day her friend will return the term of endearment, 'I love you', but until then she'll take 'ditto'. I'neta always had a hard time saying those three words together since a bad childhood experience she had with her mother. Joyce never understood how a mother could stand by while her child was being hurt.

Joyce shrugged it off and dialed Clint's number. It rang four times before he picked up.

"If you were anyone else, I would have let the answering machine pick it up," Clint said, yawning on the phone. "But only because I know you're calling to tell me your date went well, and you thank me for being the most wonderful best friend you've ever had for setting you up with this man, who is your knight in shining armor, I've decided to answer." He paused for a brief second. "I'm waiting."

Joyce laughed, "We had a wonderful time, and yes, I thank you for setting us up."

"Good. I'm happy for you. When's the next date?" Clint asked.

"None of your business," she retorted, stifling a yawn. "Stay out of this, Clint."

"And let you mess up what you and Edmund have going? You won't bet it."

"You don't think I'll stick this one through?" asked Joyce.

"Not at all. And because you admitted you had a wonderful time, I have to keep a close eye on you so you won't go running," Clint said, yawning again. "But it's late and I have to be up early for church tomorrow. Will I see you there?" Clint always found a way to throw an invitation to church, hoping one day she would take it.

"Probably not tomorrow. But, I know, one of these days I'm going to stop running," Joyce responded, mimicking Clint's voice when he was trying to convince her to attend church. "And when that day comes, Sweetie, you'll be the first to know. Goodnight."

She hung up before he had a chance to reply and rolled over. It took her a while to fall asleep but she finally did with a smile on her face.

❋ ❋ ❋

After Edmund dropped Joyce home, he decided to take a drive around town before heading home. He found himself on South Beach parking his car, then walking on sand.

How much longer, Lord?

No good thing will I withhold from those who walk uprightly.

I know that, Father, but how much longer do I have to wait? I need to find her. You did say he that finds a wife finds a good thing. I am ready, Lord.

Edmund picked up a small shell and threw it into the ocean. He watched it bounce on the reflection of the moon, and thought about his evening with Joyce. *I'm lonely, Lord.*

I will never leave you nor forsake you.

Edmund sighed then smiled. *You're getting good at this responding thing... or am I getting better at listening?*

He stood there for a while and finally headed back to his car an hour later. *I'll trust you, Father. I will.*

Edmund made this promise with so much conviction in his heart, not realizing his faith and words would be tested.

chapter 4

JOYCE WAS SITTING on her couch, back facing the arm rest, and body slouched over her bent knees. She couldn't stop laughing at the description Edmund was giving her about Clint's hairstyle back in college. This was their sixth date in two months and she was already feeling comfortable enough to have him over for dinner.

"You have to be kidding," Joyce said, wiping the tears from her eyes.

"No, I am dead serious. Clint would kill me if he knew I was telling you this," Edmund confessed.

"Oh, I have to get on him about this. A jerry curl? That would explain why he wouldn't let me see his undergrad pictures. Why in the world would he have a jerry curl in the nineties? Who does that?" She readjusted herself by slipping her legs under her bottom and facing the television.

They were trying to watch an action movie Edmund picked up, but ended up talking instead. Edmund looked at her and couldn't help smiling at the twinkle in her eyes.

"You have such an amazing smile." He brushed his hand across her cheeks and glanced at her lips.

Oh, Lord. We were doing just fine, Joyce thought to herself. She smiled at him then turned her attention back to the television. Edmund felt the tension she gave off, and sensed her uneasiness by the end of the movie. He decided to leave before he made a bigger mess of the evening.

He made a show of looking at his watch, stretched, then stood up. "I need to be headed home."

"So soon?" Joyce asked, looking at her watch. "It's only eight o'clock."

"Yeah... there's some paper work I need to get to before work tomorrow. Plus..." He gave her an apologetic smile, "I feel like I've stepped over my boundaries."

She stood up, feeling awkward with him standing over her. "Well... for a second there I thought you were going to kiss me, and... I don't know if I'm ready for that yet."

Edmund took a step closer to Joyce and cupped her face. "I would never intentionally do anything that would make you uncomfortable. I will admit I've thought about kissing you a few times tonight, but I'm not naïve or stupid. I know my limits. And with that said, I think I need to go before I really give in."

Joyce looked at him confused, not knowing what to say. He felt himself move closer and glanced at her lips again. She parted them slightly and all he had to do was lean forward to feel their softness. For a second he thought he would, but better judgment stepped in and he placed a light kiss on her forehead. He tucked her head under his chin just to hold her for a few seconds. When he felt her arms go around him, he said a quick prayer... *God, help me.*

Lord, help me. This man feels nice, Joyce silently prayed.

Edmund stepped back and smiled at her. *Lord, help me.* He found himself taking a few more steps back until the door knob was at hands reach. "I will see you tomorrow."

"So, you still want to do lunch?" She was a little afraid she may have pushed him away by not giving in. She almost felt as if she should at least give him a kiss, so he would know she did like him a little. *How long should a man wait to get a kiss?* One half of her thought. *But does that mean I should lower my standards?* The other half argued.

"Of course. I will see you tomorrow, Sunshine. Have a goodnight," he answered.

He left her and headed home thanking God he didn't give in. Half an hour later he walked into his five bedroom four bath home that his sisters helped decorate. His porcelain tiles were spotless and gorgeous but a little too much for his taste. His sisters argued he had terrible taste, so they took it upon themselves to add flavor to his humble abode. The bright chandelier that dangled from the ceiling in the foyer was definitely too much, but his sisters convinced him his company would love it. His living room was large enough to form two bedrooms and a bath, yet only held a love seat, a sofa, a recliner, a coffee table, and two end tables. A sixty inch television and a fish tank were built into the walls, causing it to look more spacious. The pool in his back yard made it easier to exercise and leave the world behind on crazy days. Especially when his mind roamed on all the things he had and the huge home he'd built with no family to share it with.

He walked into his kitchen, threw his keys on top of the island, and slung the refrigerator opened. After rummaging and deciding he wasn't hungry, he grabbed a bottle of water, and slipped through a side door that led to his home office.

This room and his bedroom his sisters weren't allowed to touch. It held all his personal things and old furniture. The cherry oak desk was new, but the black leather recliner had been his since college. He had all of his achievements hung on the wall across his desk for him to look at from time to time. Everything he'd ever achieved from first grade to grad school, in academics and sports, he hung up for his own encouragement. On a cherry oak bookshelf that stood on the left side of the room, he had pictures of his parents, grandparents, sisters, and old college friends.

He sat behind his desk and started to check his phone messages. There were two left by two out of three of his sisters reminding him to call their mother to wish her happy birthday. Another was Clint reminding him of lunch tomorrow, and the last one was from someone he hadn't spoken to in years. He had to play it twice to believe it was her.

"Hey, Edmund. This is Gloria. I know it's been a while... well, more like ten years, since we've spoken, but I'm in town for a few days on business and would love to see you. If you get this message anytime after eight tonight, give me a call. I'm staying at the BayStreet Inn. Just give the attendant my name and they'll ring you up. Hope to hear from you."

Gloria Stallmon. Gloria was the love of his life when he was in college. He met her in his Critical Theory class, and she was the one everyone disliked. She went out of her way to argue with everyone in the class just to prove a point. The two of them were always going at it, until one day she approached him after class. She stood a few inches shorter than his six foot frame. Her hair was neatly twisted in locks and her eyes were a pretty gray. Her bust line was larger than what you would expect on a slim woman, and the tight clothing she wore left nothing to the imagination. Her whole demeanor screamed trouble, and he only wished now that he would have listened to his instincts.

"You don't like me too much, do you," she asked, blocking the exit. Everyone had already left and it was just her, him, and one of his old friends staying behind to talk to the professor.

"I wouldn't say I don't like you, more like I've had it up to my neck with you."

"Good," she said, with a flirtatious smile.

"Good?" He was taken aback by that response.

"I'm getting under your skin, and that's what I've wanted to do since I first laid eyes on you. You look like the type who always has to keep it together, and I wanted to shake that. Glad I did. Now, would you like to go have lunch?"

"Even though I'm telling myself you're crazy," he responded, before giving her an inviting smile, "you're also intriguing, and I think I'll take you up on that offer."

Ever since then him and Gloria were the couple on campus. Gloria and Edmund dated throughout their whole college career— four years. Edmund believed he had found the love of his life, until she came home and announced the news. He remembered sitting on the ottoman in the living room putting together one of his trinkets, and she sitting across from him on the love seat.

I'm leaving in two months, he remembered Gloria saying.

Yeah? So you're deciding to take a cruise or something after graduation? He was half listening to her, being engulfed in his newest project.

No... I'm leaving for good. I received a scholarship to attend law school at Yale.

That's wonderful, Baby, taking one of the pieces to attach to another one.

I'm also getting married.

Well... that's a new way of proposing, but... He lifted up his head for the first time and looked at her. The way she was sitting and the look she had on her face told him this wasn't a joke. *To who*, he asked.

She shrugged, crossed her legs, and answered him, *Laron.*

Laron was Gloria's ex-boyfriend, but worst of all, Edmund's second cousin. *Why?*

He swore he saw a flash of regret and hurt in her eyes, but it quickly changed to cynicism. The last words she said to him cut him deeper than any knife could have gone. *I got everything I wanted from you. It's time to move on to better things, and from what I've heard he's suppose to be inheriting your grandfather's company. I think I'll stick with the money making side of the family.*

Four years of lies and deceit were hard for Edmund to get over. It took him a while, especially after she got married a month after telling him.

One Sunday morning in service he went up for prayer during altar call, and when he left church the feeling of rejection, anger, and hurt didn't follow him home.

Unfortunately, for Laron and Gloria, their grandfather closed the business in Connecticut, and reopened in Miami... all for the sake of handing it to Edmund. Since then, the company doubled in profit.

Thinking about it now, Edmund couldn't help but smile at how it all ended. *I would love to see her. What should I do?*

Leave it in the past.

It'll be a short conversation. I don't still love her, so nothing can happen.

Leave it in the past.

Edmund sighed and walked into his bedroom. It wasn't the answer he wanted to hear, so it must not be God talking, he thought. *I'm just going to talk with her. What harm can that cause?*

❈ ❈ ❈

With her Tweety pajama pants and T-shirt on, Joyce ran to her front door, yanked it open, and ran back down the hallway into her bedroom. Clint stepped into her brightly lit living room, and shook his head while shutting the door.

"You're not ready yet," Clint said. Making himself comfortable on her couch, he ignored the irritation building. "Come on, Joyce. It's nine forty. We're already running late."

"I'm sorry. I woke up late," Joyce yelled out from her room. "I'll be out in a few minutes."

"Which means twenty in your language." He picked up the stuffed teddy bear that sat on the couch, then looked around her living room admiring the portraits that gave it a warm feel. "You do remember we're meeting Edmund for lunch, right? So, wear something nice."

"For one, I don't need any fashion tips from you, and two, he's not meeting us for lunch anymore."

"Why not?" Clint asked, wondering why he didn't receive this memo.

"He said something about having an emergency he needed to take care of," she shouted back. "So, it's just you and me, Sweetie. You want to treat, again?" Joyce asked, with a hint of humor in her voice.

"No. You're too greedy. You need to slow down. Your pants are getting a little tight."

"So, you're looking now? You better slow your role before your girl yanks that leash she has around your neck," Joyce answered with a chuckle.

"She doesn't have a leash around my neck. If she did, I wouldn't be here right now."

Walking out of the room fully dressed in black casual pants, turquoise shirt, and black flats, with her short hair gelled down, she stuck her tongue at him and rolled her eyes. "Whatever that's supposed to mean." She dug into her purse, then glanced around the living room with a confused look. "As soon as I can find my keys, we can head out."

She found them lying on the kitchen counter and snatched them up. She walked back into the living room, dangled the keys in his face and waited for him to stand. When he didn't, she sat next to him and waited for him to talk.

Looking at the bear he held in his hands, Clint said, "Eileen and I got into an argument the other night. She doesn't believe our friendship is platonic and there's nothing going on between me and you."

Joyce waited for him to say more, hoping he would admit to having some feelings for her; but when that part of the conversation didn't come, she said, "Well… she's a woman and she has every right to be cautious. You're a good man, Clint. We don't come across the likes of you every day. And you have to admit, our friendship is kind of unique. I don't even understand it sometimes. Plus," her voice holding a mischievous tone, she smiled at him. "I am stunning. I'll be scared of me, too."

"I'm serious, Joyce. We've been dating for almost three years now, and she still doesn't trust me." He ran his hand down his face, not wanting to show how bothered he really was about this. "She tried to give me an ultimatum between you and her."

"What did you say?" Joyce asked nervously, hoping he didn't quickly give up their friendship.

"Bye!" He admitted, letting out a breath of air. "I didn't mean it and she knows that, but I'm not going to sit here and let some woman, who does not trust me, dictate who I have as friends and who I don't."

"Well… that woman is your woman. You love her, don't you?"

"And she knows that. So, why do we go through this? You're a dear friend, and I love you as a friend." Feeling frustrated, he stood up and threw the bear on the couch. "I'm telling you, if it's not you today, it's someone else tomorrow, and I don't know if I can deal with this foolishness anymore. I'm fed up with it, Joyce."

Standing up, she rubbed his back. "It'll be fine, Clint. This is what being in a relationship is all about. Just relax, take a deep breath, and smile. I have to be with you for three hours and I don't need a grizzly bear on my construction site. Thank you very much."

Clint smiled for the first time that morning, and turned to give her a hug. "Thank you."

"You're welcome," she hugged him back. *Remember, nothing but friends*, she reminded herself. "Now, this is why your girlfriend has questions. Get off me and let's go."

Clint accompanied Joyce to where the new site of her next project was being built. As an Architect that contract with companies to build buildings from the ground up, she likes to oversee how her employees were doing and make sure everything was on track. By the time it hit one o'clock, they both were starving and headed to Monty's for lunch.

Taking a sip of her water, Joyce gave Clint a thankful smile. "Thanks for helping me today, Clint. Since Frank has been sick, this new project has been driving me crazy. I need my project manager to get better soon."

"Don't thank me now. You owe me big."

"Yeah, yeah, yeah." Joyce browsed the menu as if she didn't know what she wanted. "Does your girlfriend know you're having lunch with me?"

"Nope," Clint grudgingly admitted. "And I'm not going to tell her."

"Get over it already, Clint, and stop pouting. You both been together too long to let this break you up now."

"Whatever," he said, sounding like a pouting child. He looked towards the entrance, and saw a familiar face walking in. "I guess Edmund changed his mind about meeting us for lunch."

She turned to see what he was talking about. "Well... he made a good guess about where we were eating, because I didn't tell him." She turned away, feeling as if his being there had nothing to do with her.

"Well, maybe he's on a business meeting." Clint hoped that was exactly what it was, but his gut was telling him that was not the case.

Joyce gave Clint a look that said 'nice try' and shoved her shoulders. "Maybe. But the fact that you had to say that means you feel what I feel."

She paid attention to where he was seated— three tables to her right. He sat down, with his hand folded and his eyebrows in a scowl. She saw a gorgeous woman come in, about a hundred and thirty pounds, jet black locks twisted into a bun, and hips and thighs bulging against a tailored black suit. She carried a black suitcase and walked as if she knew everyone's eyes were on her. Before she made it half way to Edmund's table, something in the pit of Joyce's stomach started to hurt, sensing this stunning goddess was here to meet the man she thought was growing to care for her as much as she was starting to care for him. Before she could conceal the hurt, she watched Edmund give Goddess a "too-close-for-comfort" hug, and she gave him a sensual kiss on the cheek. Joyce let out the breath she was unconsciously holding and gave Clint a hurt look.

Clint reached over to squeeze her hand. "Do you want to leave?"

"Yes," she murmured, picking up her purse. "I just had a sudden loss of appetite."

Both her and Clint placed a tip on the table for their water and started to walk out. By that time, Edmund saw them and Joyce risked another glance his way. The look on his face was all she needed to know this lunch date had nothing to do with business.

chapter 5

"I'LL GIVE YOU a call later, I'neta. I'm headed out for my regular morning run with Clint," Joyce said, in an attempt to end the conversation.

Her mood today was no better than it was two weeks ago when she saw Edmund with that beautiful woman. She had been trying to get off this slump by digging herself into work, but that only seemed to make matters worse. Every phone call, every knock on her door, she expected it to be him. After two weeks of no contact from him, she deemed herself an idiot and wrote him off as a jerk. Now, she was doing the next best thing to forget a man, and that was work herself into exhaustion.

"Alright. There's something I need to talk to you about. So, call me as soon as you get a chance," I'neta said.

"Yeah. Bye." Joyce quickly hung up the phone and grabbed her iPod and keys. By the time she reached her front door, her phone rang again.

She answered with more agitation in her voice than she meant to show. "I'm headed out now, Clint. I'neta had me on the phone."

"Good morning, Joyce." Edmund's nervous voice came through the line.

Oh, no he didn't. It's been two weeks, and now he calls. Joyce figured that's how long he needed to come up with an excuse. Edmund figured that's how long she needed to calm down.

"Good morning," Joyce reluctantly answered. *Why am I talking to this guy? I should be hanging up on him right now.*

"Seems like I'm catching you at a bad time."

"Yeah, you are." She dangled her keys for effect. "I'm supposed to be meeting Clint in a few. What can I do for you?" She made sure her irritation leaked through the phone for him to hear. It didn't matter that his deep voice made her ear tingle. She could care less about her physical reaction to him. If anything, she would really like to strangle that dark chocolate neck of his.

"I want to apologize about that afternoon... over dinner tonight."

What the...? "No can do. I'm busy."

"When are you free?"

"I'm not sure." She sighed aloud, hoping he really heard the irritation. "Look, there's no need for you to apologize about that afternoon."

"Were you upset?" Edmund asked.

"No." *Yes.*

"Hurt?"

She waited a second to answer, and that was all he needed.

"That is why I need to apologize. I want to explain—"

She interrupted him. "There's no need to explain anything. Have we established anything, Edmund?"

"Not exactly." His deep voice responded, sounding confused about where this question was headed.

"Do we have some kind of relationship?" she asked.

"No, but—"

She interrupted him, again. "That's why you don't have to explain. You're a free man. Free to do as you please, and whomever you please to do it with. Now, with that said, I have to go."

"Promise you'll meet me for dinner before the week is over. I would really like to see you, Joyce."

She smirked, wishing he could see it. "You don't think I'll hang up on you, do you? I told you I'm busy—"

"Tonight. But one night out the week shouldn't hurt. It'll be an early dinner, and you can leave whenever you want to."

She sighed again. "Fine. Thursday night, at six. Monty's sound like a good place. Seems like you know it pretty well."

"Ouch. OK, I deserved that one. And for what it's worth... I'm sorry."

She slammed her phone down, not acknowledging his apology. Slamming her front door and ignoring the look her neighbor across the street gave her, she headed east towards Clint's house. She ran about two miles, listening to whatever her iPod played, before she caught up with Clint. Thoughts of her ex chasing her down the street years ago, and her father chasing her with his belt made her run faster. They ran another mile before turning back to run three miles back to Clint's place.

She threw herself on the couch, while he grabbed two bottles of water from the refrigerator. Everything in her body ached and burned, but she would rather feel that than anything else.

Clint knew something had been wrong since that afternoon at Monty's. Joyce avoided him, and any conversation he struck up, her comments were short and to the point. Her run today was more intense than usual. He sat next to her and waited for her to say something. When she didn't, he spoke instead.

He leaned back against the couch and cleared his throat. "You ran extra long today," he commented.

"I needed the run," she said, taking a sip from the bottle. "Trying to lose weight." She kept her gaze directly in front of her, looking at nothing in particular.

"You okay?" he asked.

"Yep. Just have a lot on my mind."

"Anything you want to talk about?"

"Not really."

"Is it about Edmund?"

"It's about me, and I don't want to talk about it," she reiterated very sternly. Her legs started rocking, which was a sign she was getting irritated.

"OK." Giving up on the conversation, he lifted his hands in mock surrender. "I'm sorry," he said, standing up. "I'm going to jump in the shower. Feel free to whatever you want." He turned away from her, annoyed with her lack of response

"Does that include you?" she asked out of nowhere. Her eyes never moved from the spot in front of her, but her legs stopped the rocking motion.

Clint stopped midway and made his way back to her.

Kneeling in front of her, he took her hands in his. "What's wrong, Joyce?"

She finally focused her eyes on him and the look he saw scared him. "Nothing."

"The last time you made a pass at me, you were going through that break up with your fiancé..."

"Yes, I know. But I'm not now. So, what excuse are you going to use?"

He sat next to her, afraid of where this was heading. "We've been friends for how long now, Joyce?"

She shrugged and went back to rocking her legs. "Some years."

"Why now?"

"I have before." She turned to look at him and her eyes fell on his lips.

"Yeah... but..."

"You thought I was on the rebound." She slightly turned her body to face him. "It doesn't mean I've never thought about it." Her voice switched to a soft whisper.

"But..." he sighed, more confused. "I'm with Eileen and—."

"Are you reminding me or yourself?"

"Joyce, whatever it is you are—"

She interrupted him with a kiss that quickly interrupted his train of thought. When he didn't back away, she leaned a little closer and placed her hands on his shoulders. A slight shiver ran down his back and something fluttered in his stomach. For a brief second he gave into the feelings of the kiss, and tilted his head slightly. He leaned a little closer, and just when he reached to grasp her waist and pull her closer, he felt a nudge somewhere inside of him to stop.

Be careful.

Clint quickly jumped off the couch, and gave them some distance. "We can't do this, Joyce."

I can't handle another rejection, Joyce thought. Moving quickly to end the situation before he did, she stood up and grabbed her keys. "You're right. I've crossed the line and I shouldn't have."

He ran his hand over his face, visibly shaken. "Wait. What—"

She cut him off, not ready to hear what she thought he was going to say. "Don't... My mind is..." She backed away from him until she felt the front door against her back. "I've been dealing with this rejection thing again and..." She opened the door, "It's just been one of those days... weeks... months. I'm sorry."

She walked out leaving him perplexed about what had just happened between them. Worst of all, he couldn't explain the feeling that captivated him when she placed her lips on his.

✳ ✳ ✳

I'neta and Joyce were sitting in Joyce's living room, both lying across the brown couch facing each other. I'neta was painting her finger nails a fuchsia color, while Joyce was busy looking through the television guide trying to find something to watch.

"Mason had another woman at my house last week," I'neta said out of nowhere. She kept on painting her left hand as if what she said was not major.

Joyce looked up sharply, not sure if she heard right. "Say that again."

"You heard me right," I'neta said. She sat up to rest her elbows on her knees. "I ended one of my group sessions early one night because one of the ladies had an emergency, and when I got home I found him and some chick in the den."

Forgetting about the show she was suppose to be finding, Joyce gave I'neta her full attention. "In your house," she asked when she realized I'neta was serious.

"My house, Girl," she sighed, eyes glistening. "It was one of his ex-girlfriends. I wanted to hurt him so bad, but I kept my cool. I'm always telling the ladies in my group sessions it's one thing letting a man know he has your heart, it's another showing him he has control over you. I couldn't contradict that, so,

I kicked him out, even though every bit of me wanted to hurt every bit of him."

Joyce laid the remote control on the coffee table, while shaking her head in disbelief. "Wait, wait, wait, wait, wait! In your house? Why in the world would he bring another woman to your house?"

I'neta set the nail polish down and leaned her head back against the couch. She exhaled as if she had been holding her breath the entire time. "Same thing I wondered."

Joyce shook her head again. "He wanted to get caught. He's nothing but an idiot, anyway. I don't understand how a man can have a dime piece right in his hands, and turn around to exchange it for a nickel. Yeah... he wanted to get caught. Why else would he bring another woman to your place?"

"Well..."

Joyce knew that tone too well. She looked at her friend and waited for the bomb she knew was coming. "Well, what?"

I'neta exhaled for the third time in less than three minutes, like obtaining oxygen was becoming complicated. "He kinda sorta moved in with me a few weeks ago."

"Whoa!" Joyce jumped up into a sitting position and threw the remote at I'neta. "I'neta! You gotta be kidding me. Why?"

I'neta caught the remote before it made contact with her face, "That's what he wanted. Plus..."

"Has he been back to the house since?"

"No. He's called hundreds of times since then, but I wouldn't talk to him. I'm fed up with it, with him, with men in general."

"I'm sorry, Girl," Joyce said, once she realized this wasn't the time to lecture her friend. "Why didn't you tell me sooner," she asked, positioning herself to hug her friend.

"I don't know. You seemed a little distant the last couple of weeks, and... seemed like you had a lot on your mind."

"But that doesn't stop me from being a friend." She squeezed her one more time, before letting her go. "I did have a lot on my mind, but..."

"Plus…" I'neta gave Joyce a sheepish looked. "Mason caught me with Timothy."

"Timothy?! OK, this is getting to be too much." Joyce stood up to hover over I'neta on that note and was ready to give her friend a sermon whether she wanted to hear it or not. "Timothy, I'neta? Please don't tell me you're getting involved with that man again. After what he's done—"

I'neta held her hand up to cut Joyce off. "It wasn't anything like that. Timothy stopped by my office one night wanting to talk—"

Joyce interrupted I'neta holding one finger up. "It's been almost twelve years now. How does he know where you work?"

"I am in the phone book, Joyce. Aren't you just a little suspicious and untrusting of me," I'neta responded sarcastically." She stood up and started to pace back and forth, needing something to do to distract herself from the emotions trying to surface. *Come on, Girl, get it together. You don't break down… ever.* She stopped directly in front of Joyce, and exhaled one more time, "Timothy came by and I let him in for a few minutes."

"What did he want?" Joyce asked. Crossing her arms, she took her seat and waited for the excuse Timothy gave.

"Another chance, basically." She turned her back to Joyce and yanked her hair from the ponytail it was in, a sign she was feeling constricted and wired.

"Well?" Joyce knew although I'neta had common sense, sometimes when it came to men she acted like a plum fool and made very unwise decisions.

I'neta took another deep breath before facing Joyce. "Girl, please. I hope you know me better than that. I told him there is no way on God's green Earth we would ever get back together and kicked him out. But before he left he kissed me and that's when Mason walked in. He stopped by to bring me dinner. We argued for a while and he wouldn't believe there wasn't anything going on. Mason left and a couple of days later I walked in on him with another woman."

"Girl… this is a Lifetime movie," Joyce commented, shaking her head from side to side. "So, you're thinking what he did was payback for what he thought happened between you and Timothy?"

I'neta dropped herself on the couch next to Joyce. With more sadness in her voice than she intended to show, she answered, "Probably, but whatever the reason was, I don't want anything else to do with him. I packed all of his stuff and left it outside that same night. When I woke up the next morning, it was gone. So, hopefully he got it, if not, somebody's walking around here with some pretty expensive stuff," she laughed aloud.

"Are you okay, though?" Joyce asked, after chuckling at I'neta's attempt at humor. Seeing the sadness in her eyes, Joyce rubbed her back and wished she could take it all away with just one hug, but knew by experience it didn't go that way.

"I will be. Men come and go," I'neta responded, "but you, I will always have. You know you're my girl, right."

"Ditto," Joyce retorted.

I'neta shrugged her off, controlling her tears from falling. "Now, tell me what happened with Edmund."

Joyce picked up the remote and went back to channel surfing. "Well, I'll give you the short version. We made plans to go out, he cancelled because he had an emergency, which happened to be a very attractive, slim, and curvaceous woman he had lunch with at the same time we were supposed to meet. He called two weeks after the fact and asked me out to dinner to explain. Whether I care to hear it, I don't know," she shrugged in an attempt to shake off the hurt. "It was good while it lasted. Oh well." Joyce said, while staring intently at the television.

Seeing the façade Joyce was trying to hold up, I'neta took the remote from her and turned the television off. "As a friend who knows you, give yourself that much. Allow him to explain whatever that was. Dinner with another woman doesn't mean it was cheating."

"Lying about your plans, then calling me two weeks later to explain shows otherwise. Plus, we never really established a relationship, so technically he wasn't cheating."

"Yet, you were... are hurt. What else would explain your attitude this week?"

Joyce hadn't told I'neta what happened between her and Clint, and she didn't plan to.

"It has more to do with my hurt pride. I'm not even sure if I like this dude, but rejection doesn't feel good either way."

"Oh, come on. You deserve the right to have an explanation of what happened. Maybe he had a work related emergency, which didn't last as long as he thought it would."

"He hugged and kissed her, I'neta. Then called two weeks later to try and explain."

I'neta chuckled and returned the favor of the back rub Joyce recently gave her. "I hug and kiss my cousins. Give him a chance to explain, Joyce. I'm not telling you to forget what happened. Examine what you're getting upset about to see if it's really worth it."

Joyce thought about it and finally gave in. "Alright, fine. But only because I do deserve to know why he chose her instead of me."

"Gosh, you're stubborn. You can't go in it thinking like that." I'neta rolled her eyes, then turned to face Joyce and took her face in both of her hands. "You really like this guy, Joyce, first guy in years. I know it and so do you. Losing him over some assumption is not worth it, is it?"

Not unless being with him would help me get over these feelings for Clint.

chapter 6

JOYCE WALKED INTO Monty's nervous and tense, wondering why she allowed I'neta to talk her into seeing Edmund again. When she walked in, the maître d' seated her at a table hidden too far in the corner for comfort. She asked if she could be seated somewhere else but was told this was the order he received from the man who made the reservations. After bringing two glasses of water, the waiter stayed away as if he was given orders to do so. She sat there waiting for Edmund for almost fifteen minutes before he showed up.

"Nice of you to show up," Joyce said, a little perturbed. "For a minute there, I thought you'd made plans with someone else."

Edmund stared at her for a brief moment before sitting. "I'm going to ignore that childish remark."

Oh, no he didn't. "Childish," Joyce echoed, becoming angrier by the second.

"Yes, childish. I called you for dinner to apologize about that afternoon. I didn't think you would be immature enough to hold on to it this long. Yes, I was wrong for lying. I admit that. But, just as you stated the other night, we have not established a relationship." Edmund picked up his glass of water as if what he said solidified everything.

Joyce bit her tongue to control what she really wanted to say, and instead asked, "Then why invite me here to apologize? If there is no relationship, then there is no reason to explain your actions."

"I've learned there is when dealing with women. Men usually have to go the extra mile."

I don't need to hear anymore of this. She pushed her seat back with so much force it almost toppled over. "Well, let me help you lessen the mile. I'm not one of those women you feel you have to break an arm and a leg to entertain. I'm not up for playing games, wasting neither my time nor yours. And to help make sure this does not happen again," she grabbed her purse and stood up, "thank you for the opportunity of meeting you and I hope when you find the right woman, that extra mile will be worth it."

Not caring that the other patrons were now staring at her, she shoved the chair underneath the table, hoping it bumped really hard against Edmund's leg. She walked out feeling hurt and humiliated, kicking herself the entire way. *Why did I even waste my time? Daw, I'm so stupid.* What she really wanted to do was cry for allowing herself to be vulnerable. *I said I wouldn't let myself get here again, and look at me. Just because a handsome man was interested… well, must not be if he's seeing someone else. Ugh, Joyce. When would you ever learn?*

She willed herself not to cry, not until she reached the comfort of her own home, anyway. By the time she got to her car, she felt a hand on her arm. She turned to scream, until she noticed who it was.

"I'm sorry," Edmund apologized in a soft voice. "I came here defensive, and that caused me to be rude. I had a long day, and a very aggravating client, which does not excuse my attitude, but I am truly sorry."

"Oh pa-lease, Edmund. You called me here." She angrily snatched her arm away. "Two weeks after being caught with some woman. You were the one that lied, after making me believe you were pursuing only me. So, don't give me that crap about having a long day. I've had a long life." By the end of the sentence she was yelling at him.

"I did. I did do all of that, and I really want to apologize for it, Joyce."

Feeling too angry to continue the conversation, she said, "Fine, Edmund." She turned away and dug into her purse to find her keys. "Apology accepted."

He grasped her arm again. "Wait, Joyce. Would you just hear me out?"

Snatching her arm away, she turned to face him. "Grab me like that again, and you will really see how angry I am."

He lifted his hands up in surrender. "Just have dinner with me tonight, Joyce. Please." Seeing that she wasn't budging, he continued. "Come on, Joyce. Don't let that afternoon stop you from establishing what this could be."

She gasped. "Don't let...? Seriously? Did that really just come out of your mouth?" Laughing without much humor, she pointed her finger in his face. "*I* didn't end this, Edmund. You did. All by yourself."

"And I'm trying to apologize," he said, taking the hand that was pointing at him. "Let's go back inside and discuss this over dinner. Please."

His touch caused her anger to simmer down a bit. She looked at his hand holding hers, and something in her wanted to believe everything he was saying right then. Mellowing down, she looked at him confused. "Why? If we don't—"

"Because, regardless of what you think, I care about you. Just give me this night to explain who she was and why I did what I did. And if you don't want to see me again... then fine."

Joyce, you better not. All he's going to do is lie. Just say 'no'. It's as easy as that. One word. "I..." she took a deep breath, and rolled her eyes. "Until I'm ready to leave?" *That was not what you were supposed to say. What's the matter with you?*

"Whenever you want to leave is all right with me."

"All right. You get ten minutes to tell me the truth." *Help me, God.*

Return to your first love.

She paused to look at Edmund but his lips weren't moving. She looked around to see if anyone else was around, but the parking lot was empty of other patrons. *I know I heard a voice, but...*

she shook her head and figured that the voice came from one of the passing vehicles.

She walked back into the restaurant still feeling a little offended, yet pleased that he came after her. He pulled out her seat, then waited for her to sit before sitting next to her. Not soon afterwards their waiter arrived to take their orders. After ordering, Edmund sat quietly wondering how he was going to explain canceling a lunch date with her to see an ex-girlfriend.

"Gloria and I use to date when we were in college," Edmund started off saying. "Gloria is the woman you saw me with a few weeks ago."

"Wow, that's a great way to start," Joyce said, sarcastically.

"Well... Gloria and I were together for four years before she left me to be with my cousin, Laron. " He shrugged his shoulders and fidgeted with his fingers. "Before she and I got together, she was dating him. Something I was totally clueless about. Apparently, they still had something going on while we were together. She decided to break it off with me and marry him with the notion he was inheriting my grandfather's business."

Joyce was focused on what he was saying, not wanting to miss anything. "The one that you own?"

"That one, exactly." He exhaled as if it was killing him to even say as much.

Noticing how hard it was for him to speak about it, Joyce could only wonder, *Is it hard for him to talk about it because he still cares for her or because he's afraid of losing me.* "It must have been a knock across her head when she found out you inherited the company and not Laron," Joyce commented.

"Yeah. She divorced him when she found out my grandfather was relocating his business to Miami. Their marriage only lasted some of six months."

"You kept inform, huh?" Joyce wasn't sure whether that bothered her or not.

"My grandfather told me," he responded, leaning forward. "Anyway, it has been a little over ten years since I've last seen or heard from her. And when she called one night, I just had to see her."

"You just had to see her, huh?" She looked him straight in the eyes, daring him to lie. "Do you still have feelings for her?"

"No. I used to be deeply in love with this woman. And it took me a while to get over her, but once I did, I did for good. I just had to make sure, for myself. Seeing her that day was the only way I would have known." Edmund looked Joyce in the eye. "It's always easy saying you've gotten over someone that lives thousands of miles away, but the truth is always revealed when you're up close."

Not for me. I know I'm over Noel. There's no need to see him again to know that for sure. "True enough. But, why lie? Why not just tell me you've had other plans?"

"I don't know. I was afraid you would be angry and want to break this off, but I needed to see her to make sure the past was all we had."

"And what if when you saw her you realized the past was still there? What was the plan then?"

"There wasn't one. I was so sure I was over her, so any kind of attraction being there wasn't going to be an issue."

"The point of the matter, Edmund, is that you lied. People only lie when they're trying to hide something. What is it you're trying to hide?"

"Nothing, Joyce. I just didn't know how you would have handled the truth."

"You didn't give me the chance to make any decision about the truth."

"You're right, and I am sorry."

Joyce shrugged her shoulders and took a sip of her water. Her mouth was suddenly dry. "So, what of your relationship with your cousin?"

"We weren't really that close. We stayed together for the first year during college because we felt obligated to. After that, we spoke when we saw each other in passing, but that was about it."

"So..." She placed the napkin across her lap, "are you and Gloria keeping in touch?"

"No. After that afternoon, that was all she wrote. I want to focus on what we're building here." He reached across and gently grasped her hand. "And I believe she can be more of a distraction than a help."

"And what are we actually building here, Edmund?"

"I don't know, but I'm hoping this will lead to something more than friendship." He lifted up his other hand before she interrupted. "I'm not saying we have to jump on it now. Let's take it slow, and whatever happens, happens. Just note what I feel for you is something way stronger than friendship."

She gently tugged her hand away, and decided to tell him the truth. "I'm not sure that I can say the same. I do like you, but not more than a friend."

Edmund quizzically looked at her. "So, explain your response about Gloria?"

Avoiding his eyes, she looked into her glass. "It was more of my pride and ego being hurt that made me angry. I felt rejected, and that never feels good regardless of who it's coming from."

Edmund cleared his throat and attempted to mask his disappointment. "OK. I can take that. Guess I'll have to take it slow, huh?"

Joyce looked at him and smiled for the first time that evening. "Slow is good. There is nothing wrong with building a friendship."

"You are absolutely correct. Some of the greatest romantic relationships started off as friendships. But," he gladly ended the subject, seeing the waiter arriving with their salads, "we'll discuss that at a later time."

Joyce shook her head seeing how relentless he was. "OK, Edmund... we can talk about it later, but I doubt anything would change."

"And you're so sure about that? Why?"

Because I'm in love with my best friend. "Because... it's a woman's intuition."

Edmund smiled as the waiter placed their salads on the table. "Well, I hope to prove you wrong, Dear."

※ ※ ※

Clint and Eileen were sitting in his living room attempting to watch a movie, ignoring the tension in the air. Moments earlier, they were in a heated discussion about Clint's friendship with Joyce, when Clint ended it by turning the television on and ordering the first movie he saw on Netflix.

Wanting to apologize but not knowing how, Eileen moved a little closer to Clint, locking their fingers together. Without making so much of a sound, Clint gently tugged his hand away and folded his arms.

"How long are you planning on staying mad?" Eileen asked, attempting to hide the hurt through anger.

Clint shook his head and pinched the bridge of his nose. *Please, not again.* "Eileen... please. Let's finish watching this movie. OK?"

"No, it's not OK. I'm trying to apologize."

Clint snickered. "And you're doing that by starting another argument? Classic." He grabbed the remote control and increased the volume.

Eileen crossed her arms over her chest, and smirked at him. "I bet you if Joyce wanted to talk you would switch in a heartbeat."

Clint turned to look at Eileen and wondered how such a beautiful creature could be so insecure. Medium built frame, with chestnut colored skin, hair stylishly pinned up, dark chocolate eyes, and a gorgeous smile, she made heads turn everywhere she went.

Clint remembered the first time he saw her. It was one Sunday morning at Changing Lives Ministry. He looked into the audience from the choir stand and saw the enchanted look of worship on her face. Her head lifted up, eyes closed, arms lifted above her head in surrender. Her lips moved as if she was whispering sweet words to her Lord, and the peaceful look on her face said it was just her and Jesus in that place that morning. No one else mattered. The passion behind her worship was what attracted him to her.

God, what happened? Clint didn't hear a response, but he felt their relationship was the distraction.

"You know what," he said, turning the television off and facing her. "This really has nothing to do with Joyce. It's about how insecure you are. I have done nothing these past three years we've been together to make you feel that way. I have loved you and showed you in so many ways that I do. Why don't you trust me, Eileen?"

"It's not that I don't trust you, I don't trust her—"

Here we go with this same argument, he thought before responding. "Which means you don't trust my judgment of friends," he interrupted her. "This is the last time I'm telling you this, Eileen. Joyce and I have been friends for a while and will continue to be. If you can't handle that, then maybe you can't handle this relationship."

Wait a minute. She stared at Clint in disbelief. "Are you giving me an ultimatum, Clint?"

"No. I'm telling you if you can't trust me, then leave me." He sighed with so much frustration. "We've been together for almost three years. I've dealt with your jealousy, your doubts, your questions, and your insecurities, and I can't do it anymore. I could understand if I did something to make you doubt me, but I've always been faithful to you. I love you and have only loved you, but I can't take this anymore, Eileen."

"So, you're saying you don't want to be with me anymore?" Eileen's voice cracked.

"I'm saying if you can't trust me, then leave me. Three years of this is too much for any man to take. I stuck with it because I love you, but I can't anymore. Joyce will always be a part of my life, and I'm hoping you would accept that and continue being a part of mine, too. But if you can't handle the friendship we have, then maybe we need some time apart."

Eileen looked at him for a long time before nodding her head. "You might be right." She stood up, wiped her palms on her jeans, and avoided his eyes. "I'm sorry to have caused you so much grief, Clint—"

Clint stood up also. "Listen to what I'm saying, Eileen. I—"

"You're saying you want to break this off. I heard you loud and clear." She interrupted, grabbing her purse and sweater.

"All I'm saying is that we need some time apart to clear our minds on what we actually want. If you want to be with me, then trust me, Eileen."

She looked at Clint and smiled sadly at him. *What I would do to make him see what I see, then maybe...*She sighed and shook her head ever so slightly, disappointed in how this was going. "You're not actually sure who you want to be with, Clint. You're torn between your girlfriend of three years and your best friend of seven." She grabbed her keys from the coffee table, dangling them in front of her. "Tell me one thing Clint. Do you not see, at all, where I'm coming from?"

"I see it and I understand. But can't you see you have insecurities you need to deal with, and me getting rid of every person you're intimidated by is just pampering your issues and not helping them?" *Father, I just wish I could make her see the real issue. If she would just open her eyes,* he silently wished.

She sighed and shrugged. "Fine, Clint. Let's spend some time apart and see how that goes. You need this time as much as I do to figure out what and *who* you actually want. Good night, Clint." She walked out leaving him alone to try and make sense of what just happened.

I know what I want, Clint argued in his mind.

Seek first the kingdom of God and His righteousness, and all these things shall be added to you.

Clint shut his eyes trying to understand why this made him even more confused.

chapter 7

JOYCE ROLLED OVER to answer her phone after glancing at her clock and the caller ID. "This better be good, I'neta. It's five o'clock in the morning and I'm just now getting to sleep."

"Could you come over, J?" I'neta asked in a whisper.

The whimper in I'neta's voice put Joyce in alert. "What's wrong?" Joyce quickly sat up and turned on her bedside lamp. She couldn't remember the last time she heard fear in I'neta's voice.

"I don't know, but I don't feel safe here alone. I feel..." she whimpered. "I'm scared, J."

Joyce knew it took a lot for I'neta to admit she was scared. She jumped out of bed and yanked her dresser drawer open, pulling out a green T-shirt and gray jogging pants. "Of what, or should I say who?"

"Mason finally got a hold of me three nights before last during my monthly group session. I told him things were over between us, and I no longer wanted to see him," she whimpered again. "Joyce, he's been following me since. I walked out my office last night and he was parked across from me. And not too long ago, I heard someone trying to break into my house."

"Did you call the police?" Joyce asked, while pulling the T-shirt and pants over her tank top and pajama shorts.

"Yes. They searched the premises and found no one. They did see a set of footprints around the back. So, it shows someone was here. They also found my kitchen window cracked like someone was trying to break in... He's scaring me, Joyce, and I don't know what to do."

"Well... you know I'm an expert at bobbing and weaving punches," Joyce said, making a dry attempt at humor.

"That's really not funny, J," I'neta scolded.

"I'm sorry. That was a poor attempt to lighten the mood. I'll be there in a little, OK."

Joyce hung up with I'neta and slipped on a pair of socks and running shoes. By the time she walked out her door and sped to I'neta's house, ten minutes passed. Both Joyce and I'neta checked all the windows to make sure they were locked and secured. It was now going on seven o'clock and neither of them were asleep.

"I'm sorry to bother you, Girl. I know you have to be at work in a couple of hours," I'neta apologized, lying on the queen size bed next to Joyce.

"Girl, please. That's the pleasure of being your own boss. You don't have to answer to no one but yourself. I'll just call Frank and let him know I won't be coming in. He can handle things on his own."

"I've never told you this, Joyce, but... Mason hit me."

"I know," Joyce responded.

I'neta looked at Joyce surprisingly. "How?"

"I saw the signs. Remember I use to be in an abusive relationship."

"How did you do it, Joyce? How did you leave him still loving him? 'Cause although Mason did those things, my heart can't seem to let go."

"I had no choice, Net. After the last time, it was either me or him. And the fact that he killed our baby..." Joyce took a deep breath and released it very slowly, still finding this hard to talk about. "I figured if he can do what he did to me while I was pregnant with his child, there's no telling what was next. That last time was the worst of them."

Joyce remembered that night too vividly. She was three months pregnant, sitting in their studio apartment around eleven thirty that night, waiting on Noel to get home. When he stumbled in, she could smell the alcohol on his breath before she saw the crazed look in his eyes.

God, please not tonight, she remembered praying aloud. Noel heard her and decided to make it the root of their argument. It took him awhile, but he finally stumbled his way from the door, across the living room to where she was sitting. She wanted to get up because she always hated the defenseless feeling she got whenever he towered over her, but her stomach was a little bit more upset than usual that night. She grabbed her belly, which seemed to enrage him more. He picked her up by the neck and threw her across the room, toward the front door. He walked to where she was lying, picked her up, and slammed her against the wall.

She knew screaming wouldn't help in the kind of neighborhood she lived in, so she prayed. *Lord, whatever happens tonight, please don't let me lose my baby. I promise I'll leave him for good this time, if you keep my child safe.* The next thing she knew, he opened their front door, grabbed her by the shoulders, and shoved her down the stairs. The only thing that saved her was a neighbor walking by. Noel got too afraid to go head-to-head with the guy, so he walked inside and slammed the door. The guy called an ambulance while pulling her up to a sitting position. By the time she reached the hospital, she'd lost the baby.

"Do you miss him sometimes?" I'neta asked, bringing her back to the present.

"I use to. Got over that quickly, though."

"I miss Mason, J. Am I stupid for that?"

"No. You gave him your heart and it takes time to get it back. Especially if he's not willing to let it go."

"When is Noel getting released from prison?"

"He has the option of applying for probation in a few months. If it's granted to him..."

"Are you ready?"

"I don't have a choice but to be." Joyce shut her eyes to that prospect. *But I'm not, Lord*, she thought.

"He still writes?" I'neta asked, closing her eyes.

"All the time. Never misses a weekend. The last letter, he professed to be a changed man and wants to tidy things up with me."

"And?"

"No ands about it. I'm through with that part of my life. I'm just going to need all the help I can get to keep him away from me."

Look unto the Lord, from which comes your help.

I don't know if I can. It's been so long.

"I love you, Joyce," I'neta said, on the way to sleep.

"I love you, too."

✳ ✳ ✳

Clint threw off his blanket to answer the phone. Looking at his clock, he murmurs, "It is seven thirty in the morning. This better be good."

"Hello," Clint answered with a groggy, irritated voice.

"Hey," Eileen replied hesitantly.

Clint sat up in bed and slumped against the head board. "Good morning. Early morning. What's up?"

"Can I see you this morning?" Eileen asked nervously. She knew he didn't like waking early, but she needed to say what she had to say before she lost her nerves.

"For breakfast," was all Clint could ask, looking at the clock again.

"No, for dinner." *Watch it, Girl. No sarcasm, OK. That's not what this conversation is about.* "Sorry. Yes, for breakfast," she quickly retracted. "Do you have plans?"

"No, I don't, but I wanted to take this free time and clean up my place. You know how much of a mess it's in." Clint rose from his bed and stretched like a cat. He yawned and exhaled slowly.

"Well... if... maybe next time. Sorry to wake you." Sounding disappointed, Eileen was ready to hang up and forget about the whole thing.

"Wait, wait... wait, Eileen. I'm sorry. Breakfast sounds wonderful." He walked into his bathroom shaking off the grogginess. "At what time?"

"Does nine o'clock sound good to you?"

"Yeah, it does." He chuckled to himself. "I forgot you are an early riser."

"Yeah, I am. Something instilled in me as a kid."

"I take it we're having breakfast at your house."

"No. How about the Denny's on Biscayne Boulevard? Is that okay with you?"

"Yeah. That's fine. I'll see you in a bit."

Clint hung up with Eileen and thought hard about jumping back into bed for a few minutes. *This seven thirty in the morning thing is not working*, he thought. He gave one last stretch, then jumped into the shower. Pulling on a pair of khaki's, a navy blue polo shirt, and tan boots, he arrived at Denny's ten minutes early, but Eileen was already waiting for him.

"Good morning, again," Clint said, taking the seat across from her.

"Good morning. You're early." She looked a little nervous and had a hard time looking him in the face.

"So are you."

She shrugged and started playing with the sugar dispenser. "Well... I couldn't sit still at home, so I decided to come here and wait."

"Antsy about what you want to say to me," Clint stated rather than asked.

Eileen had always been amazed at how well Clint could read her. *So why can't he understand how and why I feel the way I do about this so call friendship he has with this woman?* "I never could get how you could read me so well sometimes, but..."

"I've been with you for three years," he shrugged, picking up a menu. "And based on how hard you're ringing your hands right now, I'm guessing what you have to say won't be easy."

Chuckling, she placed her hands flat on top of the table. "You really are something else." She looked him straight in the eyes. "Tell me, Clint, how do you really feel about us?"

"What do you mean?" *Haven't I told her I love her? What kind of question is that?*

Her eyes gleamed sadly as she smiled, "When you think about this relationship, where do you see it going?"

Be honest.

Honest? OK. How do I say this? "Well... I don't know. I mean... I see you as a potential wife, but... I don't know. So far, that's all I see... potential."

Eileen nodded her head in agreement. "That's our problem here. I see you as a potential husband... just not mine." She looked away from him and stared at the table. "Clint, I am thirty years old and you are thirty-two. Don't you think people our age should be courting the ones we're supposed to be with? "

"Where are you headed with this, Eileen?"

Still staring at nothing in particular on the table, she cleared her throat before saying, "After I left your house last night, I went for a ride... talking to God. I asked Him what I should do, and when I got home there was a bouquet of flowers waiting for me on my steps." She started ringing her fingers again. "They were from my ex-fiancé, Paris. I thought about how Pastor is always saying nothing is a coincidence when you're in God, and how He orchestrates things to fit His purpose. Maybe we were meant to be in each other's lives for a season, and that season... is now over."

"Maybe that is what's going on, Eileen, but remember He's not the only one hearing our prayers. Some things are sent as distractions. Didn't you tell me your relationship with Paris was... always compromising? You both were always giving way to temptation?"

Getting defensive, Eileen gave Clint a look that said she was ready for war. "You make it seem like there's no room for change. I'm sure you weren't always holy, Clint, and made a few mistakes yourself. But you've changed. You've changed within the three years we've been together. Could not Paris have done the same?"

"You're right. He could have, but...," rubbing his neck, he shook off the argument he felt brewing. "So, you're breaking this... us off completely?"

"I believe I am, Clint. I mean... our season is over. For the last six, seven months all we've done is argued and maybe it's because it's time for us to go our separate ways."

"Are you planning on examining this thing with Paris?"

"Not right now. I'm too confused for that, and I wouldn't dare bring him into this rebound stage. That would be unfair. I need this time alone to take care of me, you know." She finally gave Clint a bashful look. "Not every guy will be as patient as you've been with my insecurities."

"You're right about that," he jokingly said.

She popped him softly on the wrist. "Whatever. I know I'm not perfect and I have some areas to work on. It's gonna take some time, but hey... I'll get there after a while."

"It takes time for everyone to get where they should be. That's exactly why we need God. Without Him, you really can't move forward."

"Well... does this mean we don't see or speak to each other again?" she asked.

"No. I hope not. You were three important years of my life, Eileen. And, even if we're not together, I would like for us to still talk."

"Good," she exhaled nervously. "Well...," she grabbed her purse and stood up. "I don't have much of an appetite, so I think I'll get going."

Clint stood up pushing his chair in. "Neither do I. Guess breakfast wasn't breakfast after all."

"Guess not. Our time together was fun, wasn't it, Clint?"

"It was. We had our times, but that's part of having a relationship."

"Yeah, that's part of having a relationship. Well, guess the next time I'll see you will be in church."

"Or in passing, but... yeah. Take care, Eileen."

"You too, Clint. Goodbye."

She left without a backwards glance, and he watched her walk away. *Well, that went well. Keep her, Father, from... everything that's not you*, Clint silently prayed. He followed her lead and left the diner being very much at ease about what just happened.

chapter 8

I'NETA SAT ON Joyce's bed watching her go frantic about what she should wear on her date with Edmund. She actually found it amusing to watch her pull something out of the closet, put it on, then throw it across the room to grab something else, only to repeat the process.

With an amused smile on her face, I'neta leaned back on her elbows. "So, tell me, Joyce... where are you two going tonight?"

"Skating," Joyce answered, looking over a brown ruffled, sleeveless shirt. "I haven't been skating in over ten years, but this is what he wanted to do tonight." She flung the shirt across the room and rummaged through her closet again.

"So, you're telling me you're making this big of a fuss over clothes that's gonna get dragged on someone's skating floor? Interesting."

"I'neta, please. We may be going out to eat later and I still want to look my best." This time Joyce held a blue and white, button-down checker shirt, which she scrunched her nose at and threw across the room on top of the pile she was creating.

I'neta stared at the pile, then got up and walked over to the mess, and rummaged through a few items. "So... what's wrong with the twenty outfits you just flung over here? They all seem fine, Joyce."

"Not comfortable enough or dinner-presentable."

"You're crazy," I'neta said, picking up a pair of black leggings, a purple designer shirt, and a black belt. "Wear this, Girl. It's casual enough for skating and nice enough for dinner afterwards. Trust me, he's not making too much of a fuss like you are right now. Plus, I'm not sure what all the fuss is about since you're just friends."

Joyce took the clothes items from I'neta, "You sure?" She looked at the items as if they were growing heads.

"Positive." She stood in front of Joyce with her arms crossed, daring her to argue.

Seeing the look on I'neta's face, Joyce shrugged and said, "All right." Making her way back to her closet to grab a pair of black wedges, Joyce asked, "How about joining us?"

"Girl, please. And be the third wheel?" She plopped herself on the bed and resumed going through some of Joyce's clothes items. "I think not."

"You don't have anything to do. You can't sit here by yourself all night."

"Watch me. I'm not being a third wheel, J." She gave Joyce an adamant look, then resumed admiring a chocolate and teal halter top, placing it to the side to take home. "Maybe I'll go back to my place and straighten up some things."

"You can't go back there and you know it," Joyce said while looking through her jewelry case. "How about if I call Clint and invite him also? Would you go then?"

The last time Joyce spoke with Clint, they avoided the subject of 'the kiss'. The first few conversations were awkward, but like years before they ignored the tension. Clint shared that him and Eileen had broken up, and Joyce told him her and Edward decided to just be friends. If Clint joined them tonight, it would be the first time they would have seen each other since 'the kiss', and Joyce was nervous about how they would act towards each other.

Joyce picked up her cordless phone and started dialing without waiting for a response. "He's been locking himself in the house ever since the break up with Eileen. He needs to get out."

"Hello," Clint's voice came through the phone.

"Took you long enough to answer? What you doing?"

"Reading over some documents, Ms. Sherlock Holmes. Why?"

"Wanna go skating tonight?"

"No."

"Come on, Clint. You can't sit at home and mope around like a sad puppy. Come join us tonight. Please."

"Who's moping? I just don't want to be the third wheel stuck between you and Edmund. That is not going to happen."

"You won't be. I'neta is coming."

"I am not," I'neta said.

Joyce gave I'neta a glaring stare, then placed a finger to her lips to shush her. "Ignore that mess in the background. The four of us out would be great."

"Sounds like a double date to me," I'neta mumbled.

"You're not trying to play matchmaker, are you?" Clint asked.

"No. For the last time, it's only a date if the couple is in a relationship. Edmund and I are just friends."

"Umhm," both I'neta and Clint said in unison.

"You both listen to me. I know you two are stuck on the fact that you used to date. So, what? That was years ago. Get over it. Learn to accept that and enjoy each other's company, because I'm tired of keeping you two away from each other. We are going skating tonight, and dinner afterwards. I'll call Edmund and let him know. We will meet at Double Wheels at seven thirty. That should give you both enough time to get ready, right?"

"Yes, ma'am," both I'neta and Clint answered in unison, sounding like two students being chastised by the school's principal.

"Great. Now, hurry up. Bye." She hung up with Clint, then turned to see I'neta still sitting on the edge of the bed.

"What's the matter, Net?"

"Girl, I can't go skating with you all. I...," I'neta cut herself short and shook her head.

"If you're worried about Mason, don't. You have that restraining order against him, and it's been three months now, I'm sure he's gotten the point. You—"

"It's not that. It's..." She cut herself short.

Joyce sat next to I'neta and waited a few minutes for her to explain why she couldn't go. Joyce finally gave up on her saying anything and asked a question she's always wanted an answer to. "You know... you never really told me what happened between you and Clint. It was always a taboo topic with you."

I'neta slumped backward on the bed with a heave. Thinking about the night that changed everything for her and Clint used to make her angry, which is why she did everything not to think about it.

They were a few months into their relationship and she was attempting to give a saved guy a chance to prove they all weren't jerks. He begged her to go to a dinner party one of his friends were having, and being curious to see how Clint acted around others she agreed to go. The first few people he introduced her to were pretty decent to talk to, and everything was going well until she noticed someone she recognized. She dipped her head and whispered to Clint she had to use the restroom, hoping the gentleman did not notice her. On her way back she detoured to the kitchen and almost turned the corner until she heard Clint's voice.

"And I should believe you because...?" Clint asked.

"You don't have to believe me. Ask her. I'm just trying to help you out, Man. And from what Tim says, she can't be trusted."

Gosh, he did recognize me. She walked into the kitchen and cleared her throat. "Hello, Matthew."

Instead of responding he smirked at her, gave Clint a look of warning, then walked away shaking his head. Clint turned to look at I'neta and started to say something but shook his head.

"I think I'm ready to go. Are you?" Clint asked.

Feeling like she knew what was coming next, she put up a wall of defense and responded. "These are your friends, not mine. I'm ready to go when you are."

Clint said a few goodbyes, then they walked to the car. Instead of driving off, they sat quietly for a few minutes before he finally spoke. "Matthew... How do you know him?"

"I dated his best friend a couple of years ago," I'neta answered.

"Tim?" Clint asked, staring ahead at nothing in particular.

"Timothy, yes. It was a couple of years ago, and something I wish not to share."

Clint finally turned to look at her. "Were you pregnant with his child?"

I'neta closed her eyes for a brief second. "Yes. And yes I did have the abortion." She turned to look at Clint. "That was in my past and I want to keep it that way."

"Is what he said about you true? The stuff this Timothy told him?"

I'neta knew after she left the church, Timothy told everyone she seduced him. He told them she got pregnant from another man and tried to say it was his to get child support. And for some reason unknown to her, he lied and told others she miscarried. All of it were lies, but she had learned people will believe what they want. Looking at Clint, she knew regardless of what she said he would still choose to believe what he wanted, and based on the expression on his face he believed what Matthew said.

She straightened herself in the seat and asked him to take her home. The conversation ended there, and so did their relationship. He dropped her home and told her maybe they needed to reconsider their relationship. They both opted to end it before it got more serious.

I'neta was finally able to share this with Joyce without feeling as angry as she use to. Thinking how the conversation went then, she really didn't give Clint a chance to believe her anyway.

I'neta sat up and smiled at Joyce. "I really am fine being left alone here, Joyce."

Joyce stood up and placed her hands on her hips. "Yeah, I know. You have two hours to get yourself together."

I'neta grunted, then sighed loud and long, "Fine!" She jumped off the bed and grabbed the halter top. "I'm borrowing this by the way."

"I'm giving you until eight o'clock to meet us. If you're not there by then, I'm calling the cops. So, call or something if you're going to be late."

"I don't think Mason will bother me tonight."

"Yeah, right. And that explains why you've been spending nights over here the last few months. Eight o'clock, I'neta, or I'm making that call."

"Yeah, yeah, yeah," I'neta responded as she walked away.

"And, I'neta." Joyce waited for her to turn around before saying, "I'm glad you guys had a mutual agreement to end it. No hard feelings right?"

"No hard feelings." I'neta smirked.

She left to go home while Joyce got ready for her date.

❋ ❋ ❋

I'neta was in her bedroom going through her drawer when she heard her front door opened and closed. She kept quiet, hoping she was hearing things, but knew better when she heard silent footsteps coming from downstairs.

She grabbed her cordless phone and shut herself inside the closet. She pressed 911 so all she would have to press is the *on* button if it was who she thought it was. Kneeling on the ground in her closet and peeking through the horizontal blinds, she saw Mason walk in and took a seat on her bed, head held low with something in his hand she could not identify.

"I really miss you, I'neta. I know I was a fool for hurting you. I've been going through some things... have been going through them for a long time, and... well... it doesn't excuse how I treated you, but it would help clear things up if you would just give me five minutes to explain." He looked towards the closet waiting for a response.

She held her breath, hoping he would think she wasn't there and leave. She sat on the ground praying that this will be the one time God would hear her. *I need you, God. I know I haven't spoken to you in years, but... Right now, I need you to get this psycho out of my house. Please*, I'neta silently prayed.

"I'neta... I know you're in there 'cause I watched you come into the house, and your bedroom light is the only one on. Are you going to come out the closet so we can talk?"

Please, Lord. Would you please help me this once. You said you love me, so prove it. Get rid of him. God... I really need your help... please.

I'neta sat in the closet with her head between her knees. After a minute or two- that felt more like an hour- she heard loud stomps coming from downstairs. She jerked her head up to see Mason standing, looking towards her bedroom door, face to face with a shotgun held by a police officer. She stood up amazed, with tears running down her face. Sighing, she lifted her head, *Thank you, God.*

She stepped out of the closet to see an officer placing handcuffs on Mason, and another looking at her with relief on his face.

Erasing all facial emotions from his demeanor, the concerned officer approached I'neta, "Are you okay, ma'am?"

"Yes, I am, Officer. Thank you," I'neta confirmed, looking perplexed. "How did you all...?"

"Know? Well, one of your neighbors called and said they saw someone parked across your home the last few hours. They weren't sure what was going on, but they felt uncomfortable about the whole situation and didn't want to take any chances."

"Hmm... thank God for that," I'neta said with relief, watching them escort Mason out the room and down the stairs.

"Thank God, indeed. You're a believer?" the officer asked her.

"Well... I think I am now," she answered, finally giving him her full attention. "Long story. But tell me, how did you know that he... what made you pull out your gun?"

Clearing his voice and seeming somewhat embarrassed, he replied, "Well... I saw you when you came into the station a few months ago to file a restraining order, and... you caught my attention. So, I kind of..." He cleared his throat again, "I checked the paperwork for your address and saw that it was close to where I patrol. I figured I'll keep it in mind just in case something like this happens."

"Well, thank you very much. Thank you." Sitting down on her bed, still feeling flabbergasted about the whole thing, she stared at nothing in particular.

"If you don't mind, Ms. Villanucci, could we take this conversation downstairs?" the officer asked.

She flinched, then jumped up quickly off the bed. "Yes, of course. I'm sorry. I'm just a little... I don't know. Some of everything."

They walked downstairs where other officers were waiting out front. Mason was placed in the back seat of one of the squad cars.

"What will happen to him?" I'neta asked, turning to the officer, "Officer...?"

"Officer Mills, ma'am. Joseph Mills. He'll be booked in tonight, but will have to wait until morning to speak to a judge about posting bail."

"Which he'll probably make," Joyce said fearfully, never taking her eyes off Mason. "What will keep him from coming back once he posts bail? Because he will," she said, turning her attention to Officer Mills.

"There's no way we can physically keep him from returning, and it's obvious the restraining order doesn't mean anything to him. Is there anyone you could stay with for the time being? Someone he doesn't know?"

"Somewhat. My best friend. That's where I've been staying for the past few months. He knows about her, but they've never met, so he doesn't know where she lives. Although, I'm sure he can easily find that information." She sat on her couch, and pulled her hair loose from the neat ponytail.

Joseph sat on the arm rest of the couch. "What about any relatives out of town?"

"I'm not leaving. I'm not going to allow some man to change how I live."

"OK. Well, the one thing I can do for you is keep you under surveillance. Have my people check your home and your best friend's from time to time."

"Thank you." She leaned her head back and took a deep breath, closing her eyes.

Joseph couldn't help but stare. *Lord, she's beautiful.*

And hurt.

"Behold, I will bring it health and healing; I will heal them and reveal to them the abundance of peace and truth," Joseph whispered.

I'neta sat up straight as if she was punched and looked at him. "What did you just say?"

"Just thinking out loud," he replied, feeling uncomfortable under her stare.

"But what did you say?"

"It was a scripture that popped into my head. That's all."

"Are you a minister or something?" she asked.

"No, I'm not, and the way you asked that question makes me afraid to know what you'd have done if I was."

She swallowed and smiled trying to break the tension. "I'm sorry. Just had a bad experience once with a minister. Not something I care to relive."

"Well, I'm sorry about that." He avoided her eyes by looking at his pad. "Umm... I have to get on with my work. Are you sure you're okay?"

"Yes... I'm fine. Just a little shaky, but fine." She stood up and walked him to her door. "Thank you, again, Officer Mills. I don't know what I would have done."

"You're welcome. I will need your best friend's information so we can keep an eye out for him over there too."

"Yes, of course. Her name is Joyce Nickerson and she stays..."

She gave him the rest of the information including both her number and Joyce's. She also received the dispatch number and his personal cell. She grabbed a few of her belongings and called Joyce to let her know she had changed her mind about skating. *God, I know we have to talk. I'll do it tonight as soon as I get a chance to be alone. Thank you.*

She jumped in her car knowing that after that night, nothing in her life would ever be the same.

✳ ✳ ✳

"I can't believe Mason was bold enough to walk into your house." Joyce was pacing back and forth in her room when I'neta walked out of the bathroom, already dressed for bed in a white tank top and yellow pajama pants.

When I'neta called Joyce and told her she wasn't going skating, Joyce knew something was wrong by the sound of her voice. She called Edmund and Clint and cancelled plans. There was no way she was going to leave her friend alone, knowing something was wrong. And she was glad she didn't, because once I'neta told her what happened, she knew I'neta would have not been comfortable all alone in her place, no matter how hard she protested and wanted Joyce to go out. It was now an hour later and Joyce was getting angrier by the second.

"Why are you still on this?" I'neta asked. "It's over and done with. The idiot is in jail, and I'm fine."

"But you could have gotten hurt. Who knows what he was planning to do."

"You're right. But I thank God I didn't get the opportunity to find out."

Joyce stopped in her tracks and stared at I'neta. "Did I just hear you say God without your favorite suffix? With a 'thanks' before it?"

"You did." Ignoring her friend's stunned expression, she grabbed a pillow from Joyce's bed.

"Wow. Mason must have put the fear of God in you."

"He must have, but I'm not complaining. I'm going to sleep on the couch tonight..." She walked out of the bedroom, shutting the door behind her before Joyce could respond.

Wrapping herself in a quilt, I'neta laid on the couch and stared up at the ceiling.

God... I don't know where to start. So... I would like to say thank you for saving my life today. Thank you for hearing me this one time I needed you. Thank you for life, although life can suck sometimes. And I really thank you for not holding against me these past couple of years not speaking to you. I was really hurt from what happened with

Timothy. I didn't understand why you would allow me to go through a thing like that. I felt somewhat betrayed and alone.

After a few minutes of silence, I'neta whispered, "I loved you, God… and I thought you loved me."

With all the hurt and disappointments resurfacing, all I'neta could do was cry. But the tears had a way of soothing her soul, because after falling asleep I'neta woke up a few hours later feeling much lighter, hearing a small voice whisper, **I never left you or forsaked you.**

chapter 9

I'NETA SAT IN her living room floor sorting through her memory box, and trashing old pictures and letters from past relationships. She knew it was time to say goodbye to all the guys she's ever been with, good and bad. After that night with Mason, she realized it wasn't healthy to hold on to the past.

While looking at a picture of her and Mason, her phone rang. She froze for a brief second before answering it.

"Hello," I'neta answered apprehensively. She wasn't sure what to expect since Mason escaped from jail and the authorities had not yet found him.

"Good afternoon. Is Ms. Villanucci available?"

"This is she. How can I help you?" Not recognizing the voice, she released the breath she was holding.

"This is Officer Mills. Joseph Mills. I'm not sure whether or not you remember me..."

"No, no. I do. Is something wrong? Has Mason been found?"

"No... he hasn't been found yet... unfortunately. But we do have an All Points Bulletin out on him, and a few of our men patrolling your area and your friends'. Have you heard from him?"

Blowing out another gasp of air and slouching against the couch, "No, I haven't but I did get a few restricted calls the other night. I chose not to answer."

"Well, maybe the next time you get one of those calls, answer to see whether it's him and see if you can get some information about where he is."

"So, now you want me to do your job? What exactly are you getting paid for?"

Joseph was surprised by the humor he heard in her voice. A deep chuckle resounded in her ear before he responded. "Surveillance, ma'am."

"Hmm. Sounds like my old neighbor across the street got you beat on that one too."

"Well, people like you and her come in handy at times. We surely do need the help." He listened to her soft chuckle and thought, *I could get use to that sound.* "Well, I really just wanted to make sure you were okay and see if there was anything you needed."

"No, I'm good. Thank you for checking up on me. By the way, has someone patrolled my neighborhood today?"

"Someone should be around every hour. Why? Have you heard anything suspicious?"

"No, just wondering. I would really like to go outside and take a walk, but I don't know whether that would be safe with Mason being out and all."

"Well, if you would like, I could accompany you."

Did he just...? Na, he's just being polite. "That was a generous offer, but I would hate to put you out the way like that."

"It's not out the way at all? As a matter of fact, I'm not too far from you. I can be there in fifteen minutes."

Fifteen minutes? She looked around her living room, then down at herself. "Umm... how about thirty?"

Hearing the hesitancy in her voice, he decided to play it smart. "Thirty is good. How about you meet me at the park a block away from your house, near the bookstore. You know which one, right?"

"Yes. That would be perfect."

"Great," he said, hoping she heard the smile in his voice. "See you in a bit."

"All right." *Why do I have butterflies in my stomach?* "Goodbye." She hung up the phone and ran upstairs into her closet.

What do I wear? I don't know what to wear. She pulled out almost every outfit she could find and still wasn't satisfied. *I don't have any clothes to wear.* She picked up the phone and decided to call Joyce.

"Hello," Joyce answered.

"OK, I have to meet someone in half an hour and I don't have anything to wear. What do I do? I can't meet him in this T-shirt and sweats I have on," I'neta said frantically.

"First, you need to calm yourself down. Relax, Girl. Secondly, you need to tell me who this guy is you're meeting and where."

"It's Officer Mills."

"The guy with the handcuffs that saved your life that night? You didn't tell me you were seeing him."

"First, I don't know how to feel about handcuffs added to your description of him," she giggled, "and secondly, we're not seeing each other. He just called not too long ago... but I'll explain that at another time. Right now, I need to find something to wear."

"Well, you shouldn't be pressed for clothes. You have a mall in your closet. Where are you guys meeting?"

"The park down the street from my house." I'neta yanked out a pink and white paisley shirt and stared at it for a brief second, before flinging it on her bed. "We're supposed to meet in thirty minutes."

"Wear some jeans and a shirt. If you're headed to a park, you know it's not anything fancy. Keep comfortable."

I'neta thought about it for a while, and nodded in agreement as if Joyce could see her. "I guess. No big deal, huh?"

"No big deal, Girl. Just relax and enjoy yourself. Don't get your hopes up too high cause this could just be a friendship thing."

"Girl, please. A relationship is the last thing on my mind. Mason gave me enough to think about for the next couple of years."

"So, why are you nervous? You're over there freaking out about what to wear to a park. I bet you're snatching clothes out your closet and throwing them on your bed."

Taking a look at the few items she'd thrown on the bed, she shook her head at herself. "Because... I don't know. But I'm not looking for a relationship, Joyce. Believe me when I say that."

"Um-hm. As long as you remember that when you see those handcuffs," Joyce retorted with a giggle.

"You are unbelievable. I'm not paying you nor those hand-cuffs any mind. I'll talk to you later. Gotta get dressed."

She hung up with Joyce and pulled on a pair of low riders and an orange UM T-shirt. She brushed her hair neatly into a ponytail and slipped her feet into a pair of white Nikes. Instead of driving to the park, she decided to walk since it was a beautiful day out. The weather was perfect for kite flying and the birds were singing like they were part of a TV sitcom.

She passed by a group of women and decided to play it safe by sitting at one of the picnic tables near them. Sitting so close she was able to hear their conversation, from corn-developing shoes to nagging men. She heard a few giggles and heard one say, 'I'll love to sop him up with a biscuit'. I'neta looked up to see who the woman was referring to and was stunned.

With the fear of that night gone, she was able to see Joseph Mills in his real stature. Gone was the police uniform, but in its place was a tan polo shirt, baggy blue jeans, and brown boots placed over a six feet, two inch, two hundred pounds figure. Gone was the stern look, but in its place was a light-skinned, medium built, wide shouldered, baby face man she was happy to lay her eyes on. His smile seemed to out shine the sun once he spotted I'neta.

Just once do I wish to find the right guy. God, no more games. If he's not worth my time, let me know as soon as possible, I'neta silently prayed.

Just then she remembered a scripture, 'He who finds a wife finds a good thing...'

OK. Well, Lord, just once do I wish for the right guy to find me.

The women threw I'neta envious stares as Joseph made his way towards her. One woman sighed in disappointment when he finally reached her.

"Well, hello, I'neta. I can call you I'neta, right?" Joseph asked, sitting next to her and leaning back against the table.

She smiled at him. "Under the circumstances, I say it's not just OK, but it's also necessary." *Gosh, he's making me feel nervous.*

"I agree." He gently took her hand and pulled her up with him. "Would you like to go for a walk, and," looking at the other women, "stray away from prying eyes and ears?"

I'neta heard giggling after Joseph's comment and smiled at the blunt ease dropping they were receiving. "I guess we can. If privacy is your kind of thing."

Looking towards the group of women, Joseph smiled and gave a slight wink. "Sorry, ladies, have to take this one on a personal walk."

They giggled as Joseph and I'neta walked away. They walked in harmonious silence for a few minutes before making small talk.

"So, I assume you go to church?" I'neta asked.

"I do. At Free Worship Center. I've been there for ten years now."

"Longevity says a lot about a man."

"Well, thank you… I think. What about you? Do you attend church?"

"No. I haven't in almost ten years, and please don't ask why. It's kind of a sensitive subject."

Taking the warning for what it was, Joseph changed the subject. "So… the restraining order says you're twenty-nine years old. How long have you been in Miami?"

"Almost eleven years now. How old are you?" I'neta asked.

"I am thirty-five," he responded. "You look great for your age, by the way," he complimented.

I'neta blushed. "Thank you."

Joseph smiled at I'neta, enjoying her blush. "It really is a pretty day out, isn't it?"

"It is. I feel like I'm on a TV sitcom with the birds chirping and people jogging around me. I'm not use to this kind of…" she paused, at a loss for words.

"You're not use to this kind of peace."

She considered what he said, then nodded in agreement. "I guess that's the word I can use. I never felt this peaceful before. It's like," she looked up at the sky to find the words she was looking for to explain how she felt, "knowing that life is complicated and hard, but not worried about the outcome." She looked to Joseph, "I feel like I should be, but I'm not. You know what I mean?"

"I know exactly what you mean. That's what peace is."

"I've never really had that. Since I was young, it seemed like if it wasn't one thing it was another. My father going to jail, my mother cheating on my father, my cousin…" Stopping herself short, she realized she was about to share too much personal information. "It's like I never really had a childhood."

"A lot of us don't get the chance to enjoy our childhood. When we mature faster than our age it tends to toughen up a spot in us that's hard to break once we're adults," Joseph responded.

"Yeah, I guess that's what happened to me. I was a bully at the age of six." She chanced a look at him, "Can you believe that? Tiny ol' me, a bully." She snickered at the thought. "I had some help, though," she said, beginning to reminisce about her elementary days.

"I remember when Joyce and I first met, we couldn't stand each other. Every day we were at each other's throat and somebody had to pull us apart. Then one day, sitting in in-school suspension, we found out we both loved to read romance novels." She looked at Joseph. "I know. A six-year-old reading romance novels sounds ludicrous, but I told you I never really had a childhood, and neither did Joyce. Well… we started to talk about love, or what we thought love was, and from that day we hit it off. We would bully the other first graders and dared them to tell anyone. Awful, huh?"

"Very." He shook his head in mock disappointment. "You should have been ashamed of yourself. You and this friend of yours."

"Well, I wasn't. Don't know if Joyce ever was, but I got older and over it and hopefully some of my classmates did as well. I mean, who would remember a bully from first grade?"

"Oh, you'll be surprise. I remember this one time, while on duty, my partner and I got a call about a disturbance in a quiet neighborhood. We went to check it out and sho' nuff we heard loud arguing. Sounded like two men. I knocked on the door and a scared little girl, maybe four or five, opened it nervously. I told my partner to place her inside the squad car while I go check what's going on."

Joseph paused for a second before continuing. "I walked into the living room, and kneeling on the ground was a man, with another guy standing a few inches away from him. As I got closer, with my gun pulled out, I saw the guy standing with a knife in his hands. I looked at the guy on the ground and realized the legs of his pants were cut off and he was kneeling on cut up glass. Well, to make a long story short, the guy on the floor used to be a bully and the guy with the knife was one of his old classmates. The guy with the knife was charged, of course, and is still serving time. He stated he never regretted doing what he did until the old bully apologized to him for what he did in high school." Joseph turned towards I'neta. "So, the moral is, you never know the lifelong effect bullying could have on a person until they have a knife at your throat."

She stared at him for a while before responding to him. "See, I *was* having a peaceful day until you went and said all of that."

Joseph burst out in laughter and shook his head. "Sorry to mess up your mood."

She smiled in return and resumed walking. "No you're not. Anyway, I doubt we did any sort of damage to our classmates then. Mostly all of us became friends in high school."

"Well, that's good. Unusual to hear, but hey," Joseph responded. "So, how long were you and this Mason guy together, if you don't mind me asking?"

That was a quick change of topic. "Hmm... almost a year. I don't know why I got involved with him in the first place." She glanced at Joseph to see his response. "I mean, I know why I was first attracted to him, but don't know why I stayed with him that long."

"Once you get tied up with a person it's hard to break the bond. Especially, once the person becomes a part of you and things you said you wouldn't do or take, you find yourself doing *and* taking."

"Sounds like you're speaking from experience," I'neta observed.

"Yeah. I got myself tied up in a relationship a while back. It lasted some years, but the girl wasn't right for me. I finally broke it off, and man, did it hurt. That girl was everything I ever wanted physically, mentally, all that good stuff."

"So, why'd you break it off? You caught her cheating?"

"No. She just didn't have the spiritual attributes I needed," Joseph responded.

"And how long did it take you to figure that out?"

"I knew it since the beginning, but always made excuses for her. You know, 'Lord, she'll make it around to serving You'; or 'She needs me in order to get saved'. Little excuses that justi- fied me being with her and ignoring what God told me to do from the get go."

"So, you knew you weren't supposed to start a relationship with her?" I'neta asked.

"Yeah. The Lord warned me before I even knew I was attracted to her. I just decided to ignore the warning," he admit- ted, shaking his head. "The price I paid for disobedience was not worth any of the good times she and I shared. If I knew then what I know now about the process of cutting someone out of your life after choosing to bind yourself to them, I wouldn't have even thought about it. I know that every break up hurts, but that one had nothing to do with the break up. It had all to do with God teaching me a lesson about disobeying Him," shaking his head, he thought about how his life was then. "Never again, though. He never has to worry about me going against His will. My only answer for Him is 'Yes, Lord' and 'When'."

"So, how did she take the break up?" I'neta asked.

"Not too well. She couldn't understand if everything was going so well between us, why I wanted to break it off. She didn't understand it was a matter of spiritual life and death," Joseph responded.

"Well, there are some things Christians understand better than those who are not. You knew better but she didn't. Seems like you were more to blame for dragging her into it."

"Don't I know it. I've felt guilty about it for months before I forgave myself."

"You should have," I'neta said, her face turning from pleasant to angry.

"What? Forgave myself?"

"No. Felt bad. She got hurt because you decided to ignore the fact that God knew what was best for you. You were careless about the overall effect it would have on her. Which was kind of selfish, if you ask me."

Looking at her oddly, he tried to figure out the change in her mood. "Which I came to realize during the process of us breaking up."

"Yes, but not soon enough." She picked up pace, leaving him behind.

"I'neta, wait. You're making this seem like I had a personal vendetta against this woman." He lengthen his stride to keep in pace with her.

"Might as well. What you did was selfish and inconsiderate and..." At a loss for words, she stopped herself short.

"And regretful," he admitted, gently grabbing her hand. "I've apologized to her, to God, and... to her, numerous of times. There's nothing I can do to erase what I did."

"Exactly! You didn't stop to give thought as to why God didn't want you with her in the first place. Did you ever think that maybe you weren't right for her? Probably not. You decided to oblige yourself with whomever you pleased. Now she has to walk around dealing with the damage you've caused," she responded heatedly.

God, what is going on? Joseph looked at I'neta and saw the fire in her eyes. He watched her chest rise and fall from her hard breathing.

It's not you she's seeing, it's him.

Still holding her hand, Joseph said, "I'neta, I'm not that guy who hurt you. Whoever he was, I'm sure was a jerk—"

She interrupted him. "Stop. You don't know him and you would probably never know the damage he caused." She slipped her hand from his. "And as far as I'm concern, you might as well be him."

She looked away from his misty eyes and exhaled heavily. She turned to him and for a few seconds he thought he saw regret in her eyes, but it was quickly replaced with determination.

I guess he's not the right one, Lord.

"I believe we'll call this the end of our walk, Joseph. Thanks for the company."

"So… wait… you're ending our afternoon because of a past mistake that clearly had nothing to do with you?"

"Yes, I am!" Her response was a little sharper than she intended.

"So, as soon as you hear something you don't agree with, you run?" Joseph was a little confused and a tad bit upset. *This is ridiculous.*

"No. As soon as I see someone who's able to put me in the same predicament my ex did, I run."

That hurt, Lord. "Well, sad to see that a woman of your caliber would be foolish enough to box all men in the same category with your ex. I guess we'll call it an afternoon. Would you like me to see you home?"

"No. It's still day out and there are too many people out for anything crazy to happen." She looked around and realized they were back at the table where the small group of women sat.

"Looks like there was some progress made there," I'neta said sarcastically, bringing his attention to the women. "And none here."

I'm not taking any more of this. "None at all. I'll walk you to your car." He turned away from her, making his way to the parking lot, but stopped at her next remark.

"I didn't drive. It was too pretty out. I decided to walk instead."

Turning around to look at her as if she'd lost her mind, he said, "That wasn't wise. Especially, with Mason out on the run. I think I should give you a ride home."

"And I think you should not." She sighed and looked at him with regret again. "Look, Joseph, I'll be fine. My home is less than ten minutes away and it's still daylight. If it would make you feel better, you can follow me in your car."

"I'm not a stalker. Either I walk you home or drive you. Those are the only two choices you have."

She saw the stubborn look on his face and realized he wasn't changing his mind. "Fine. You can drive me. But you will not be coming in." She walked pass him with her head held high.

"That's fine. I'm more concerned about your safety than your friendship," he replied, catching up with her.

She gave him an annoyed look and walked ahead of him to the only squad car she saw. She watched him walk to a dark grey Chrysler 300 and unlocked the passenger door.

"I don't use the patrol car on off days," he said while holding the door open.

"My assumption." She gracefully slipped her slim figure into his large car. The short ride to her home was full of tension and she hated feeling awkward around someone she really knew nothing about. She wanted to apologize for her reaction earlier but knew it was too late. He pulled up to her home and she stepped out without one more word. By the time she entered her house and locked the door, he was already gone. She was not sure why but she felt unhappy about what had just happened.

chapter 10

Joyce was in her office wrapping up her last project when her secretary buzzed her phone. "Yes, Ms. Ruby?" Joyce mechanically answered her secretary of three years. She had been pleased to work with her since she started her architectural firm. Although Joyce was her boss, their relationship was more so of mother and daughter.

Ms. Ruby first took the job as a volunteer when Joyce's previous secretary, Ms. Ruby's granddaughter Jessica, got married and had to relocate. While others bit their tongues, Ms. Ruby never held back her thoughts about how Joyce treated an employee, a colleague, or a customer. Her bluntness and honesty were the only reasons Joyce placed her on payroll, and her work was superb.

"It's six o'clock, Ms. Nickerson," Ms. Ruby reminded Joyce. It always tickled Joyce how Ms. Ruby would try to get formal when no one else was around, just to bring a point home.

"Thanks, Ms.Ruby. Give me about thirty minutes and I'll be out."

"Listen, Boss. You've been working nonstop since six thirty this morning. You need to get some food in your system. I suggest you leave now and worry about all this mess tomorrow," Ms. Ruby said in a no non-sense tone.

"I did have something to eat. You brought me that tuna sandwich a few hours ago," Joyce said, focused on her computer screen.

"I brought you that sandwich seven hours ago. Go on home, Joyce. This project will be here tomorrow."

"Just thirty more minutes, Ms. Ruby. I'll leave soon after that."

Ms. Ruby paused for a brief second, then exhaled long and hard; which usually means she was giving in. "You young folks are unbelievable. Well, just make sure you stop somewhere and grab you some dinner. Knowing you, there will be no cooking when you get home," Ruby ordered.

"Yes, ma'am, will do. You're headed to see the grandkids?" Joyce asked.

"Yes, yes. Them two children are my pride and joy. Well, of course including Jessica."

"How is she and her new husband doing? I haven't heard from her since she was here last Christmas?"

"Oh, she's great. Good and pregnant. Found out last night I'm gonna be a great grandmother. She did tell me to tell you hello. Says she's glad I was able to take over when she left. She don't know what you would have done without a stable hand here to help you."

Chuckling, Joyce took her eyes from the computer screen and looked at the phone like Ms. Ruby could see her. "She's beginning to sound more like her grandmother. Tell her I said congratulations. And tell them cute grandbabies of yours I said hello."

"Why don't you tell them yourself? You haven't been by to see them in a while and they really miss you, Joyce."

That comment wiped the smile from her face, and she leaned her head back against her chair. "You know how things been busy around here, Ms. Ruby. You know I would love to see those children if I could."

"Yes... I know you would. Just letting you know they miss you. I'll make sure to tell them you're thinking about 'em. Have a goodnight, Joyce."

"Goodnight, Ms. Ruby."

Joyce heard the line disconnect and the front door opened and closed soon afterwards. Fifteen minutes later she heard the front door opened again, and saw Ms. Ruby's head poking through her door.

"Knowing you, I figured you weren't going to stop for dinner, so I decided to stop by the deli across the street and get you something to eat," Ms. Ruby said, pulling Joyce's attention from the computer screen.

"Thank you, Ms. Ruby. You shouldn't have." She poked her head around her computer to give Ms. Ruby a smile.

Ms. Ruby returned her smile and responded, "My pleasure. My pleasure indeed." She looked behind her and as soon as she did, Edmund walked in.

"Hey," he said bashfully.

Joyce face lit up in surprise. "Hey, yourself." She noticed Ms. Ruby smiling from ear to ear. "Where did you find him?" Joyce asked her.

"At the deli. Seem like he had the same idea I had. Just beat me to it."

"Thank God I did. I couldn't have someone beating me in buying dinner for my dear friend," Edmund said, setting a picnic basket down on top of the conference table that sat to the far left of Joyce's desk. "Even if it's you, Ms. Ruby."

"Of course not, Dear," Ms. Ruby agreed. "You two have a great evening. Don't stay here too late," was Ms. Ruby's last remark before she walked out.

Edmund sat himself at the table. "How was your day?"

"Long and busy," Joyce said, turning her computer screen away from her, "but it's about time for me to call it quits." She stretched and peeled herself off her seat to see what he had in the basket. "This was pretty nice of you, Edmund."

Edmund pulled out a container of red beans and rice, sweet plantains, fried fish and side salad. "It's not a big deal. I was near the area and knew you'll be here late."

"Smells like you went to my favorite restaurant."

"It was on the way."

Edmund pulled out the knives and forks that came with the plates, while Joyce went to the vending machine and got two bottles of ice tea. She sat next to him and they ate in companionable silence.

In between bites, Joyce found herself staring at Edmund, wondering where all of this was going.

"So... I really don't know anything about your childhood. Feel like sharing?" Joyce asked in order to generate conversation.

"Sure." Edmund took a drink of his tea and wiped his mouth. "Well, my three sisters and I were fortunate to be raised by both of my parents. My mom was a school teacher and my father, deciding not to take on the family business, was an editor for a major magazine. Both are now retired and living very well. My mother is also an evangelist at Great God Fellowship Church up in Connecticut, and my father is a deacon."

"So, everything for you was pretty normal, huh?"

"I guess. We had our family issues. No one is exempt from those, but we stuck together like a family should. All three of my sisters are married with children. My mother is just ready for me to do the same. You know how that goes."

"Yes, I do. 'When am I going to get some grand babies from you? I'm not getting any younger. Will I ever get to see my precious daughter get married and have children of her own,'" Joyce said, mimicking her mother. "I never hear the end of it."

"So, you can imagine how I get it being the first born and the only son. I have the responsibility of keeping the Devereau's last name alive."

"Well... you are the only son."

"I am that."

They settled back into companionable silence, both in their own thoughts. They ate like that for a few minutes before Joyce asked the taboo question.

"Heard from Gloria lately?"

He coughed, then cleared his throat. "No. Where did that come from?"

She shrugged and started to pick at a crumb on the table. "Well, it's not like I don't know about her, Edmund. You can tell me. We're just friends."

"No, Joyce. I haven't seen her since that day… months ago. I was serious when I said I wanted to pursue something with you."

"Edmund, my response still hasn't changed. I only see you as a friend. Can't that just be enough?"

"It can be… for now."

She looked him in the eye, and shook her head. "You're so relentless."

"I am." He took Joyce's hand in both of his and gave her an innocent smile. "Look, I know you're afraid to get into a relationship. But why don't you just give us a chance? I'm not talking about marriage, Joyce."

Joyce looked at him and saw the serious look on his face. *Well, this is the first guy I've spent so much time with since Clint. Friendship is a good way to start a relationship. Maybe I can grow to like him in that way.*

She blushed at the way he was intently looking at her. "OK, Edmund. I will give this a chance."

Kissing her palm and restraining himself from doing more, he smiled wide enough to make her laugh. "Yes! We'll be great together." He looked at his watch and saw that it was getting late. "Come on, I'll help you clean up this mess and lock up."

They locked up after Joyce made sure the computers were shut down. She turned on the security light and activated the alarm. Edmund walked her to her car and helped her in.

"Thank you for dinner tonight, Edmund. That was very sweet of you," Joyce said while starting the ignition.

"My pleasure. So… you're headed home?"

"Yeah. I think I'll take a shower and pop a movie in to clear my mind of today's work," she said.

"Sounds good," Edmund said, clearing his throat. "I have to head back to the office to grab some documents."

"Always working, huh. Well, you're welcome to come by afterwards to watch a movie with me," Joyce invited.

He looked at his watch to avoid more eye contact. "I can't. I would love to, but too much work to do." He dipped his head inside her window to give her a kiss on the cheek. "Maybe some other time." He tapped the roof of her car and turned away before she could reply to his refusal. He walked a few yards to his car, while she sat there watching him through her rearview mirror. As soon as he got near his car, she drove off.

Edmund jumped into his SUV and felt uneasy about his next destination. *I'm just meeting an old friend. Nothing more to it.*

✳ ✳ ✳

Clint was in his kitchen placing the last few dishes inside the dishwasher, while bopping his head to a new gospel rap CD one of his friends bought for him, when there was a knock at his door. He placed the dishrag in the sink, wiped his hands on a kitchen towel, and walked toward his living room. Without looking through the peephole, he yanked the door open. To his shock he found Edmund standing in his doorway.

"Well, hey. What's up, Edmund?" *And why do you look a mess?*

"Nothing much, you mind if I come in?" Edmund asked as he walked in, not waiting for an answer.

"Naw, naw. Make yourself at home." Clint stepped back to let Edmund pass by and shut the door. *This doesn't feel right. Something's wrong,* Clint thought. Looking at Edmund, Clint noticed his pants and dress shirt were wrinkled, with a few missing buttons.

Edmund sat down on the couch with his face in his hands, and Clint sat across from him waiting to hear what was wrong. They sat for a few minutes in silence before Clint stood up to turn the music off and grab something to drink.

"Would you like something to drink?"

Edmund lifted his head for the first time since he walked in. "A cup of water would do. Thanks."

Clint got him a glass of water and waited for Edmund to say something.

"I saw Gloria again last night," Edmund started off, looking at his folded hands.

"Wow. Did she show up at your job again?"

"No, Clint. I saw Gloria," Edmund said again, this time looking Clint right in the eye.

Clint shut his eyes for a second, "Why, Edmund?"

"I don't know. I mean… one minute I'm reminding myself why calling her back would be a bad idea. The next minute, we're at a coffee shop talking about what use to be. How did I get into this, Clint?"

He didn't listen.

"You didn't listen," was Clint's only response.

"What do you mean, I didn't listen?" Edmund asked, puzzled.

"Well, the first time God told you not to get involved, you ignored Him. Usually, after ignoring Him the first time, it becomes a little easier."

"I know," he sighed and leaned back staring at the ceiling. "It just got out of control. It's like… she had control over me. I couldn't say no to her."

Clint felt like there was more to this story. "What happened, Edmund?"

"Well, while at the coffee shop she asked if she could see my new yacht. Wanting to show off what I've accomplished since she walked out on me, I took her to the bay and gave her a tour. By the time we made it to the bottom deck near the bedrooms she worked herself up to kissing me."

"And you let her," Clint asked, a little worried.

"Let her," he snorted. "I wanted her to." He shook his head and rubbed the back of his neck. *I never thought I'll be in this situation. I should have just listened.*

"What else happened, Edmund?" Clint asked, feeling there was more to this than just a kiss.

Edmund sat up straight, swiped his hand over his face, and stared at his hand. "Way too much."

"Please don't tell me you…" Clint couldn't even ask the question.

"No. We didn't have sex, but we came very close to it."

"How close?"

"Clothes almost coming off, touching, fondling close. Nothing happened, but something happened. We came too close and the sad part about it, Clint," he said looking at him, "I wasn't the one to stop."

"Wow, Man. Look. We all make mistakes and do some crazy things, saved and all. But the great thing about being saved is you feel convicted, get a chance to repent, are forgiven, and never have to go back to that sin again. Truth be told, this will not be the last mistake you make."

"You're right, and I know all of that. I still chose to be disobedient and I was the one to get myself into this mess," he smirked. "I wasn't even the one to stop before it really got out of hand." Running his hand across his face, he grunted into it. "I'm the saved one, Clint, and I was the one that lost control."

"That's why God told you no from the get go. He knows there are some things you still haven't mastered yet and He tried to keep you away from it. Listen next time."

"I also lied to Joyce. I brought her dinner, and when she asked me to come over to watch a movie, I told her I had to do some work. She even asked me if I'd seen Gloria since the last time she saw us together, and I told her no."

Clint ignored the weird feeling in his chest. "I thought you were just friends? What does it matter?"

Edmund smiled sadly. "I asked her last night to give us a chance and she agreed. We are officially dating."

Clint swallowed the anger and some other emotion he didn't want to examine. "Well... the only thing I can tell you is the truth will be found out. You can decide how she hears this. What happens after that, I really can't say."

"Man, Clint, I messed up. Big time." He admitted, leaning back against the couch. "And knowing Joyce, there is no third chance. I screwed up and I'm afraid of the consequences."

"Consequences always follow disobedience. It's inevitable, but you still have to tell her the truth. Better that it comes from you."

He swiped his hand over his face again. "I know. I just don't want to lose her, you know what I mean? I care for her too much to put her through another heart break."

"Should'a thought about that before you agreed to see Gloria. Pray about it and ask God for the right time to tell her. Just don't wait too long, because, honestly, there will never be a right time to hurt someone."

"Could you... would you..." Edmund took a deep breath and continued, "Would you mind praying with me right now?"

Clint understood how Edmund felt. He, too, made mistakes and was grateful of how many times God was willing to forgive him. So, he bowed his head and began to pray aloud for Edmund.

"Lord, I come before you today, on behalf of Edmund. We thank you for your grace and mercy. For your unfailing love you continue to show us in spite of our unfaithfulness at times. Forgive us for everything, Father. Forgive us for lying, fornicating, lusting, and for disobeying you. We know there are consequences behind disobeying you; we just pray that you won't take your spirit away from us. Help us to be strong, Father. Help us to give up those things that so easily beset us. We know that everything is a choice, so help us to choose to be holy and live holy. Help us to understand there is no more condemnation concerning us. Help us to not beat ourselves over the head with this situation, nor allow the enemy to do the same. We also pray for Joyce, Lord. We pray that you would strengthen her. This will not be easy for her at all; we just ask that she would use this opportunity to turn to you. Keep her, Lord, away from danger. Save, heal, deliver, and set her free. It is in your power that we pray. Amen." Clint finished the prayer and stood up.

"Amen." Edmund kept his eyes shut and head bowed, feeling like there should be more said. He continued praying in his heart. *I'm sorry, Father. I repent of what I did, and it will not happen again. I love you, Lord. I really do, regardless of the mistakes I keep on making. Please forgive me. Please.*

Edmund opened his eyes and looked straight at Clint. He blinked back a few tears then stood to give his friend a hug.

"Thank you so much, Man," said Edmund.

Slapping his back while returning the hug, Clint replied, "What else am I here for? Are you alright."

"Yeah. Just gotta face the music with Joyce."

"Yeah, well… I'll pray God's peace on that one. 'Cause that girl is liable to cut you."

"I know. You wanna join us for dinner tonight?"

Clint shook his head quick, "Nope. You're on your own with this one."

"Yeah." Edmund looked at his watch. "I have to get going. As you can tell, I slept in the yacht. I need to get home and shower, and catch up on some work before meeting Joyce tonight."

"Alright, man. Know that I'm here if you need me," Clint reassured him.

"Thanks a lot, Clint. I really do appreciate your friendship."

"Anytime, man, anytime. I'll holla at you later."

Clint closed the door behind Edmund, then turned the music back on to drown out the questions nagging him about the emotion he refused to examine.

chapter 11

WHAT AM I thinking, I'neta asked herself as she walked into the old white precinct. She stopped in front of the entrance, observing the chaos around her. On her left was a man sitting behind a counter, speaking on the phone, which seemed to be ringing incessantly. To her right, there was a guy handcuffed to a chair saying something about flying cows to another man sitting directly in front of him. In front of her, other officers walked back and forth as if it was the national holiday of crimes. She turned towards the guy on her left and waited patiently for him to get off the phone with what seemed like a hysterical woman.

He motioned that he would be just a minute and rolled his eyes at the continuous chatter on the other end. I'neta smiled at his impatient, yet sympathetic response. She turned to lean against the counter, when she saw him walk in.

She allowed her eyes to travel from the smile on Joseph's lips to the shine of his black shoes. *Lord, this man is so handsome. Please don't let him turn me down.* He was speaking with another officer and almost walked passed her if it wasn't for her sudden sneeze.

"God bless…," Joseph cut his courtesy short once he looked up and recognized her. "God bless you." He quickly recovered and nodded his head with the intention of walking past her.

She reached out to touch his arm, "Joseph, can I… I need… I would like to talk with you for a moment."

He looked at her for a second then turned to his colleague and murmured something. His colleague smiled, gave her a once over, then walked away.

Turning to give her his full attention, he asked, "How can I help you? Has Mason showed up at your home, again?"

"No. Do you mind if we go somewhere...," she looked around at the crazy scene, "a little more private?"

"Sure. We can go in the staff room. Follow me." He walked away without a backward glance to see if she was following.

As she walked behind him, I'neta noticed the stares and heard murmurs from a few of his co-workers. They have never seen Joseph with a woman before, as he kept his private life separate from his work life. Joseph stopped in front of a glass door, opened it, and stepped aside for her to proceed. I'neta poked her head in seeing a vending machine on the far left corner, a table with a microwave, coffee machine and a box with scattered donuts on the right side of the room, a refrigerator directly in the back, and a table with six chairs in the middle. She walked in with a soft 'thank you' and sat at the first chair she could reach.

Before entering the room himself, Joseph turned towards his colleagues and said, "Slow your horses, guys. This is not what you think. I'm just an officer helping out a civilian. Now, quit staring." He closed the door behind his co-workers' laughter and sat across from I'neta. From the way he was staring at her, she felt a little nervous about why she was here.

With a slight note of irritation in his tone, he asked, "Well, Ms. Villanucci? How can I help you?"

Seeing that he had the right to be upset, she prepared to start off apologizing to him, but nothing would come out of her mouth. She cleared her throat and tried again. "I wanted to apologize for how I treated you a few weeks ago. I had no right to say the things I said and to... um..." *Why is he staring at me like this?* "I should not have compared you to my ex. I was wrong and I'm sorry."

He looked at her for a while before saying anything. "Is that all?"

She looked him in the eyes, "Yes, Joseph. I came here to apologize. I'm sorry."

"You came to apologize? After, what? Three weeks?" He pushed his chair back. "I have gotten over that, Ms.Villanucci. I hold nothing against you. I made the mistake of trying to pursue a woman who has been scarred to the point of not trusting a man, and I shouldn't have. So... your apology is accepted, but not necessary." He ignored the hurt look on her face and stood up. "And if that's all, I need to get back to work."

She looked up at him towering over her, thinking this was not going the way she had planned. *He was supposed to smile, accept my apology, then ask me out on another date. I would say 'yes'... Who am I fooling?*

"No, that's not all, Joseph. I was also hoping you would allow me to cook for you this evening. Maybe... around eight o'clock?" *I swear he can hear my heart pounding. I know he can.*

"Dinner?" Joseph considered it for a few seconds then gave his answer. "Thank you for the offer, but I don't think that'll be a good idea."

She stood up slowly, not quite understanding his rejection. "Why not?"

"Because," he sighed and rubbed his eyes. "Because I don't have the energy to go through... this. I've been through enough and though I may find you very attractive, I would rather skip that episode with you."

"Look, Joseph. Someone once told me you don't turn your back on something worth having. Regardless of how unreachable it may seem. All I'm asking for is a chance to make up for my outburst. You had to think I was worth that for you to pursue me."

"Why? What has changed your mind about me?" Joseph asked.

"Well, after you dropped me off that day I felt terrible about how I treated you. I sat down and thought about what could have reminded me of him..." She mustered the courage to look him in the eye, "and I couldn't find anything. Not one single thing. I then realized I was more afraid of letting any man that close to me again," swallowing the fear his look was provoking, she reached over to take one of his hands. "That's why I turned you away, but that's also the reason why I'm here. So, would you do me the honor of joining me for dinner tonight?"

Joseph paused for a long time giving her a blank stare. He wasn't sure what to say and he wasn't sure what to feel. He slid his hand away and turned away from her for a second. He turned to face her and saw how nervous she was.

"I can't, I'neta."

That's the first time today he's called her by her first name, but everything in her went cold. *He can't? Why not?*

"Why not?"

"I'm seeing someone else."

I'neta's legs couldn't hold her up anymore so she sat down. All she could do was stare at her hands to avoid eye contact with him. *I am such a fool. How could I think...? That's the problem. You didn't think. All right, get up and leave while you have some dignity left.*

I'neta stood up and grabbed her purse without looking at Joseph. She knew he watched her every move. "I'm sorry for wasting your time and..." She chanced another look at him before turning away. "I'll be out of your way."

She walked out and all he could do was watch her go. He shook his head and sat down at the table. *Man, I don't know what I just did but... it had to have been the right thing. Right?*

❈ ❈ ❈

Edmund checked around his place to make sure everything was in order. *All right, Lord. I'm not sure what to do when she gets here, but I'm putting this all in your hands*, he silently prayed. He looked at his watch and realized she would be arriving in less than ten minutes. He couldn't be still at all. This was the first time in a long time he was nervous about a relationship. He stood up and walked back and forth too many times to count before his doorbell rung.

Taking a deep breath, he opened his door with a tense smile on his face, "Hello, Joyce."

"Hey, Edmund. Sorry to be late. I got held up at work," she gave him a kiss on the cheek, then walked in as Edmund made room for her to get by. She threw her purse on top of his coffee table, sat down on his couch, and ran her hand through her hair before folding them on her lap. *There goes that nervous tick again. OK... breathe. Relax.*

She looked around his place trying to keep from looking at him, although he stood at the door a little longer than usual. He didn't tell her what this talk was about, but his stance by the door and his nervous expression gave her a weird feeling it wouldn't be something she liked.

Moving away from the door, he still didn't sit next to her but stood behind the love seat across from her. He looked at her for a few seconds with regret in his eyes, before hiding it with a smile. "Would you like anything to drink? I have fruit juice, water, tea."

"Oh, no thank you. I'm not thirsty." She watched him walk back and forth before softly saying his name. "Edmund."

He froze wondering if she already knew. "Yes?"

She tapped the cushion next to her. "Sit down and tell me what's bothering you."

He looked at her and felt even more like a fool. He spent months pursuing her, and when she finally agreed to date him he does something dumb.

He sat next to her knowing everything would change after this. Not having the guts to look at her, he rested his elbows on his knees and stared at his hands and whispered, "I lied to you last night."

She hesitated before responding, "About Gloria," Joyce said.

"Yes, about Gloria." He exhaled a deep breath, sat back on the couch allowing the soft cushion to hold his weight. "I saw her again... and..." He couldn't bring himself to tell her everything.

"You saw her last night, too, didn't you? Instead of going to your office, you went to see her?" Joyce knew what the answer was, but she still didn't want to hear it.

"Yeah. I don't have an excuse, Joyce."

She heaved a sigh and leaned back on the couch, staring at the ceiling to avoid looking at him. "Yeah, I know. You guys usually don't." She sounded more disappointed than angry. "Well, I can't totally blame you. You're still in love with her, wh—"

He sat up straight, cutting her off, "I am not still in love with Gloria, Joyce. I haven't been in years."

She gave him an offhanded look. "Edmund, why else would you agree to see her? Why else would you choose to end something that hasn't really started yet?"

"I don't know. I wasn't thinking, and I am sorry. I'm sorry for starting our relationship out this way."

Joyce smiled sadly at him, and patted his hand. "Sad to say, Edmund... you did not give us enough time to build a relationship. I knew I was right for keeping this a friendship." She stood to give herself some space. "You know, I really thought you would have been different from the other guys, since you're saved... but every man has his flaws."

"I do have flaws. Yes, I'm saved and that's what makes me different. That's how you know you can believe what I promise—"

"Like before," she interrupted. "After you were caught the first time, what did you tell me, Edmund? Or was that too long for you to remember? Maybe her beautiful looks and lovely figure distracted you."

Joyce asked the question that always bewildered her. "What is it with men and gold diggers? Why do you automatically flock to women who are just out to use you? Is that what I must do to get a man? Lie, cheat, steal, and be greedy?"

"No, Joyce. Be the caring, stubborn, strong-willed, loyal woman you are. I made a dumb mistake, and I'm sorry." Edmund stood, wanting to do something but not knowing what.

"Look... in all honesty, Edmund, I only gave us a try in hopes of one day growing to like you more than a friend. What happened between you and Gloria just proves you have more to work on, and getting into a relationship is not a good idea right now... for you or me."

Joyce grabbed her purse from the coffee table, and turned towards Edmund. She looked at the fear in his eyes before walking over to give him a gentle hug. "I don't hate you, Edmund.

Neither am I angry. I am a little disappointed, but not so much that we can't be friends."

She leaned back to look at him while her arms draped around his waist. "I enjoy spending time with you. There is nothing wrong with having a good friendship."

Edmund squeezed her close and softly kissed her forehead. "I guess you're right. I would rather have you as a friend than out of my life."

"I agree. So... let's just write this off as a minor mistake and think of it no more." She squeezed him one last time before letting him go. "Good night, Edmund."

Edmund watched her walk out and thought, *For a woman who is not saved she has more wisdom than I do.*

chapter 12

"Yes, Mom, all the doors in the house are locked. We go through this every time we talk, could we not go through it today? Could we please just have a normal conversation, for once?" I'neta asked, feeling a little frustrated.

"Well, shoot me for caring. Some psycho man, that doesn't know when to call it quits, is obsessed with my daughter who, by the way, lives in a huge house by herself, and I get called annoying, aggravating, frustrating, and everything else in the book. What else is a mother suppose to do when she's thousands of miles away from her daughter?"

"I love you for caring, Mom, but you've called me four times within the last two hours checking on my locks, and it's only six in the evening."

I'neta stood in the middle of the kitchen, holding a glass of water, and staring out her window. *Why couldn't you care when it mattered, Mom? Are you concern now because you feel guilty about what happened back then?* The questions I'neta had in her mind for years came drifting back, and again she suppressed them. She rubbed her eyes and swallowed the anger and hurt that usually follows. No longer thirsty, she poured the water in the sink and made her way into her living room. Throwing herself on the couch, she prepared herself for the guilt trip her mother would attempt.

Her mother sighed. "I'm just nervous because Antonio and I are not able to be down there to protect you. We do pray for you, but still… parents have the right to worry."

"How is my stepfather," she quickly asked, taking the opportunity to change the subject. "Where is that crazy man?"

"He's fine. He's out back messing with that stupid dog. I don't know why he insists on keeping that old pit bull anyway. That thing is on its last leg and—"

"Well, he's had Charlie since he was in college. Charlie's family to him," I'neta said, interrupting her mother. "Maybe I should get a dog. A small shaggy one."

"I guess you're right. I really think it's going to break Tone's heart when that dog finally does pass away," her mother said, sounding deep in thought. "Hey, has that cop, Joseph, called you yet?"

Rolling her eyes like she usually does when her mother brings Joseph up, she quickly said a prayer that her mother would let this go. *God please.* "No. And I'm not really expecting him to. I really think I've messed this one up, Mom."

"Well… a little time to yourself won't hurt you none. Maybe God has it this way so you can spend more time getting to know Him and not some man. If I know one thing, it's that God loves His time. So, what He does is take away those things that seem to get in His way of doing that, and if it's a man, then the man has to go. Just don't make the same mistake I did, Honey."

"What mistake was that, Mom?" I'neta asked, curious about what her mom was about to say next. She knew it had nothing to do with her father. Mom never spoke about those days, hoping everything would stay buried.

"After getting so comfortable with it being just me and God, I begin to lie to myself and say I didn't need a man. The more I said it, the more Antonio was in my face. The more Antonio was in my face, the harder I said I didn't need a man. I was happy being single, all by myself. Of course, that was the stubborn, independent side of me talking. Finally, God had to slap me across the head and tell me to stop being selfish."

"Well, old ways are hard to break."

"And what do you mean by that?"

Hearing the hurt and defense tone in her mother's voice, I'neta quickly gave herself a mental slap. *I gotta work on not saying the first thing that comes to mind.* "Only that being independent is a hard life to leave," I'neta said, hoping her mother will accept this explanation and not dig into the real reason why she said that.

"Hmm... that's true enough. But when the time comes for you to break out of it, you'll know."

I'neta was never able to take relationship advice from her mother. So, to control the sarcastic remarks running through her mind she reached for the television remote, made herself more comfortable on her couch and channel searched. "Well, I'm not ready for that any time soon. I'm enjoying this time to myself. I would like to find a nice church to go to, though."

"Didn't Joseph mentioned he goes to church?"

"Gosh, I swear I tell you too much," I'neta chuckled. "He did... but... I don't know how he'll feel about me coming. I've actually thought about it a few times, but... I don't want him to think I'm stalking him."

"Don't worry about all that. Go and see how you like it. If you're not comfortable, then you know that's not the one. I say go and check it out." She stopped to mumble something to someone. "All right, Baby. Antonio needs some help getting up the stairs. Looks like he hurt his back again fooling around with that dog."

"All right, Mom. It was really good talking to you. I'll call you in a couple of days. Tell Antonio I said hello."

"Will do, Baby. Make sure you lock up and check your windows."

"Mom!"

"It's my right to worry," her mother responded with a smile in her voice. "Love you, Baby."

It's a little too late for that. "Ditto. Bye, Mom." I'neta hung up with her mother and walked upstairs to her bedroom. *I think I feel like a movie tonight.* She searched her closet for something comfortable to change into, while calling the AMC Theater for shows playing that day.

✳ ✳ ✳

Dressed in light blue jeans, a white blouse that hung off one shoulder, green pumps and green jewelry, I'neta walked into the theatre. After approaching the ticket booth and ignoring the attendant's flirtatious looks, she haphazardly stuck the ticket in her back pocket, and went to purchase a box of Raisinets and small Coke. Forgetting the theatre number her movie was being shown, she dug in her back pocket for her ticket but came out empty handed. She dug her hands in her other pockets with the same result. *Where could I have placed that thing so quick?*

"You dropped it," a voice said from behind her.

She turned to see who spoke and got tongue tied. "Well, hey. I..." *Breathe, Girl.* "I didn't know I dropped it." She looked on the floor in an effort to avoid looking into Joseph's penetrating eyes. "Where is it?"

"You dropped it coming in." Handing the stub to her, he brushed her hand with his fingertips and ignored the awareness between them. "Took me a while to decide whether to pick it up or not. When I saw you, I thought I could avoid running into you," he finished, shrugging his shoulder.

Wow, that hurt, she admitted to herself. "Well, sorry to inconvenience you, but thank you, anyway." She turned away and headed towards the back, hoping she was going the right way.

"But I realized this would be my opportunity to talk to you again, and I didn't want to miss that," Joseph said.

I'neta stopped in her tracks, and slowly turned around. Looking passed the tough exterior, she noticed the nervous look in his eyes and realized there was more to what he was feeling than what he was showing. "What did you just say?" she asked.

"I said, I didn't want to miss this chance to talk to you. I kind of..." *Man this is harder than I thought.* "I'm sorry for how I treated you the last time we spoke. I was upset and wanted you to know it," he admitted, taking a step closer. "But I haven't stopped thinking about you."

Taking the chance she wouldn't have before, she took a step closer to him. "Funny you should say that because... I haven't stopped thinking about you. I've been getting involved in little things to keep from doing that, but..."

Joseph took another step closer, smelling the fruity scent of her perfume and minty breath. "I know exactly what you mean. Regardless of how hard you try, it's inevitable."

"What's inevitable?" I'neta voice caught, lost in the intense look in Joseph's dark brown eyes.

Joseph's smile reached his eyes for the first time. "What I feel for you, of course."

I'neta was so close to closing the small space left between them, and allowing her lips to do what it wanted to do since she saw him. Forgetting the other patrons walking by, the attendants at the cash registers, and the noise drifting around them, she slightly leaned towards him. Small shivers rushed up her spine, butterflies danced in her stomach, and her lips ached from wanting his kiss when the look in his eyes intensified.

Reaching to play with a small strand of hair that fell from her clip, he softly brushed her earlobe and smiled at the shiver she tried to conceal. He leaned a few inches closer, and his gazed drifted from her eyes to her lips. The sigh he released brushed her cheeks before he took a step back.

Joseph cleared his throat and looked away, while I'neta giggled nervously and looked at her movie ticket.

Getting a grip on his emotions, Joseph took another step back. "I noticed we're watching the same movie. What do you say we watch it together?"

I'neta smiled, glad that he broke the intense pressure lingering. "I'd like that."

They walked into the theater and sat through ten minutes of previews. Things were kind of awkward, and there wasn't as much talking between them. By the time the movie was over, it was an hour and forty-five minutes later, and both were relieved and nervous. They walked out of the theater in companionable silence until they reached the door heading to the parking lot.

"That was a pretty good movie," I'neta said to break the silence.

"Yes, it was," Joseph answered, looking around. "Where did you park?"

"Not too far from here. A couple of spots away."

"I'm downstairs." Not wanting this time to end, he asked her, "How about we go grab a bite to eat?"

"Umm... sure. I'm not that hungry though." *But I would make myself munch on something since you asked.*

"I know a place not too far from here. I love their Caribbean meals and they have a lovely fruit salad. Maybe you can entertain me while I have a late lunch?"

"You wouldn't be talking about Ma'Mi's would you? That's the only place I know, so far, that has the best Caribbean cuisine you will ever taste."

"That's it, exactly. How did you find out about it?"

"By accident. I took the wrong turn one day off the express-way and figured I could drive my way back to South Beach. I got hungry and ended up stopping at Ma' Mi's. Ever since, whenever I feel like Caribbean food, there is where I go."

"Awesome. Well, guess there's no need for you to follow me. I'll just meet you there."

I'neta nodded in agreement and walked to her car. Joseph watched her get into her car and walked the two flights to his. *How weird of you to put us together like this, God. What are you planning here?* With no response to his question, he shook his head and said a quick prayer, *Well... guard my heart, Lord. Please, guard my heart... and hers.*

❋ ❋ ❋

"How are you enjoying your fruit salad," Joseph asked I'neta, in hopes of clearing the tension hovering above them.

"Pretty good." She avoided his eyes, silently giving herself a pep talk. *Don't look at him. Do not look at him, I'neta.* "I'm trying to figure out this different taste. They've added a different fruit I haven't had before."

"Let me try it and I could probably tell you." He reached over and handed her his fork, which she quickly took from him and poked the weird fruit in front of her. He gave it a bite and the look on his face changed from curiosity, to pleasure, then to recognition. His mouth slowly moved and she could imagine his tongue maneuvering the piece of foreign fruit in his mouth. *Wow, he has such beautiful lips.* She shook her head and redirected her gaze to her fruit bowl. *Girl, I told you not to look at him. This is not a date, so shake it off, I'neta. Shake it off.*

"I know what this is... papaya. A Caribbean fruit, of course. Ma'mi must have just started serving this. It's pretty good. Not at all sweet or bitter." He looked at I'neta and smiled. "Perfect."

Girl, he's talking 'bout the fruit. The fruit!, she warned herself.

"Glad you liked it," she said, placing her fork down.

"I take it you didn't?" he asked

"Oh, no, I do... I just... I really wasn't hungry," she said, wiping her mouth with a napkin. "So, what are you doing coming out to the movies by yourself?" *I hope that's not too personal.*

"I needed a break from real life for a moment. This is how I usually relax. I could ask you the same. What are you doing out by yourself?"

"I needed a break and I couldn't take being cooped up in the house anymore. Felt like I was losing my mind staring at the four walls." She risked another look at him. "You wanna know what's so weird? It's like, I could feel Mason thriving on my fear. Feels like he knows I'm scared and he uses that to... I don't know. It's just weird."

"In a perverted way, he uses that as strength. He still has control over you if he can keep you from doing what you really want to do. That's how it usually goes with domestic violence. The violator—

"Excuse me, Sir." Joseph looked up to see a waitress standing next to him. "I'm sorry to interrupt your meal, but there is a gentleman outside, beating on your car with a bat."

"What!" Joseph quickly jumped up and ran outside. By the time I'neta caught up with him, she saw his gun drawn and a gray Sudan speeding off.

"Jesus Christ of Nazareth!" Joseph yelled, staring at his car. "I didn't even get the chance to see his face."

"Maybe the waitress did," I'neta said, walking towards his car. She could see the damage from the door and cringed at the mutilation. "Wow! Who would have wanted to do this to you?"

He looked at her as if he had forgotten she joined him here. "Well, I don't know. Let's see… maybe that crazy lunatic ex-boyfriend of yours," Joseph sarcastically replied.

"Yeah, right. Let's not forget you're a cop. Out of all the people who could have it in for you, Mason is the only one you could think of? That's perfect."

"Defending him, are you?"

"Whoa, don't go there, Joseph." She calmed her rising temper by inhaling and exhaling a few breaths. "I'm sorry this happened to you, but it wasn't my fault, so please… let's not spoil this lunch with unnecessary bickering," she said, looking at his car instead of that scary expression on his face. "Whoever it was didn't do too much damage. You have a busted tail-light, a few dents on your door, two flat tires, and a few cracks on your window. These things can get fix within days." She stepped closer and took his hand. "So, let's call AAA, finish our lunch, and I'll give you a ride home."

"Why? So, he can return and beat your car in?" he sarcastically asked, snatching his hand away.

"No, because I was enjoying myself with you. If this was Mason's doing, I am not going to allow him to destroy my life. I refuse to give him that much power. Now, if you don't want to finish lunch here, we can always take it back to my place."

"I rather you take me home," he answered, walking away from her. "I'll call AAA and the cops, make a report, then we can get going. In the mean while, you should probably wait inside while I stay out here to ask some questions."

"Joseph?" she called him without budging from her spot.

He turned with anger gleaming in his eyes. "What?"

"Why are you acting like this? Why are you treating me as if I'm the one who's done this?"

Control, Son.

Ignoring the voice, he closed the gap between them. "Let me ask you a question. How many times did he hit you, treated you like trash, before you left him?"

Stunned at his outburst and too embarrassed to give an answer, I'neta just looked at him.

"That is why I'm upset with you. If you would have dumped the fool the first time he laid his hands on you, this probably wouldn't be happening." Joseph voice went up an octave with every word he said.

"Wait just a minute. Are you blaming me for that fool hitting me? And for what he just did to your car, if it was even him?"

Joseph grunted and turned away. "Just get inside, I'neta, before this idiot gets back. I don't want to have to worry about you."

"Wow. Sorry to be an inconvenience to you, Joseph." Walking back into the diner, I'neta was pretty upset. She walked into the restroom, paced back and forth, and wished she had never ran into Joseph. *How could he, Lord? How could he blame me for what that idiot did to me?* She got teary-eyed but refused to let them fall. *Why did he even invite me to have lunch with him if this is how he feels about me? Why? And why am I even waiting on him? I should just let him worry about his way home.* She stayed in the restroom for about fifteen minutes before Ma'Mi walked in.

"The tow truck has arrived and your friend is ready to leave. He asked me to come for you," Ma'Mi said, approaching I'neta. "He didn't mean those things he said. Men can sometimes be hot headed and say things they really don't mean."

"Ma'Mi, the Bible says, 'Out of the abundance of the heart the mouth speaks.' If he wasn't feeling those things he wouldn't have said it. Plus, it really doesn't matter. This wouldn't have worked out, even if I wanted it to."

"He cares for you, Sweetheart. You can tell by how he looks at you. That's why he can't understand why you would have let a fool touch you like that. It's not you he's upset with, it's the idiot."

"It's okay, Ma'Mi. It really is. I'm harder than you think I am, and it takes more than a man's opinion to break me."

"Even if the man is important to you?" she asked.

"Especially, if the man is important to me." She walked out with her head held high and Ma'Mi shaking hers.

By the time I'neta made it outside, Joseph looked like he was under control and apologetic. He looked at I'neta but knew this wouldn't be the right time to say anything. She unlocked her car doors and jumped in without giving him the chance to hold it open for her. The only thing she asked for and wanted an answer to was his address.

The tension was thick and Joseph swore if she had a knife she would opt to cut him. He admitted to himself, once he calmed down, that he shouldn't have said nor treated I'neta the way he had. *I'm sorry, Father. I just hope she's willing to accept my apology*, he prayed.

She pulled up in front of his home, amazed that the lawn was trimmed and the flowers were kept. She unlocked the doors to signal him to get out.

"I'neta—," Joseph began.

Keeping her face forward, she shook her head. "Don't. I don't need your apologies. Just get out my car, please."

"I'm really sorry."

"I really don't care. Would you please just get out my car?" She refused to even look at him.

"I was an idiot and out of line for the things I'd said," Joseph continued.

"Wow, you're still talking." She finally gave him the attention he wanted. "Well, since you're in a talkative mood, tell me why did you invite me to have lunch with you when you feel that way about me?"

"The things I said is not how I feel about you, I'neta. Nowhere near it. I was angry and stupid, and said some angry stupid things."

"So, you become verbally abusive when you're upset? Then what's the difference between you and Mason?"

That hurt. "I'm not Mason. I'm not abusive and I would never hurt you the way he did."

She gave a dry laugh and shook her head. "This was really an eventful day, Joseph. It's time for me to go and I would very much appreciate it if you would get—". Joseph cut I'neta's sentence short by softly brushing his lips across hers.

Brushing his lips one more time across hers, he leaned back an inch or so. "I'm sorry, Sweetheart. For everything. I don't blame you for what Mason did. That situation is something I won't probably understand, but I do know fear would have you make some crazy decisions. Please forgive me," Joseph whispered, mere inches from her lips.

I'neta was still in shock from the kiss and didn't know what to say. She closed her eyes and thought about the rush she felt when Joseph placed his lips on hers. *I didn't know a simple kiss could feel that way.* She opened her eyes to see his lips moving but she couldn't hear anything but the rush of blood in her head. *What is this man talking about and why is he not kissing me again?* She started to inch forward when her common sense kicked in. *Girl, think about this before you get into this. Think about it hard. Yes, his lips are softer than they look, but that doesn't change how he just hurt you.* She shook her head and backed away from him until her head hit the window.

"I think you should leave now, Joseph." She turned her head so she wouldn't have to look at his lips again. "Please get out. I accept your apology. Just get out." She grasped the steering wheel hard enough to make her hand pale and waited for him to close the door before she locked them. She inhaled and held it for a few seconds before letting it out. *That still didn't calm my nerves.* She sped off before he even got a chance to say goodbye.

chapter 13

"Ms. Nickerson, your ten o'clock appointment is here," Ms. Ruby buzzed in.

"Thank you, Ms. Ruby. Go ahead and send him in," Joyce reached over to pull the new client's file to refresh her memory of his project. She stood up when she heard her doorknob clicked. Ms. Ruby preceded the man in. With a slim figure perfectly shielded in a charcoal colored suit, black hair slicked back into a ponytail, and face shaved clean, he resembled the actor Antonio Banderas.

"Good morning, Mr. Mariano. It is a pleasure to finally meet the face behind the voice," Joyce welcomed her client in with her hand stretched out.

He shook her hand and gave her a salacious smile. "Yes it is, Ms. Nickerson. We finally meet after playing phone tag for two weeks. I must say, the face is even more beautiful than the voice."

"Well, thank you." She blushed from his obvious flirting, but made eye contact with Ms. Ruby to not encourage anymore. "Thank you, Ms. Ruby. I'll take it from here."

After the door shut, she waited for him to take his seat before she took hers. "From what we have discussed on the phone, you're looking to build a restaurant near Aventura."

"That is correct," he responded.

"You do know that area is very competitive. There are already a dozen restaurants I can tell you off the top of my head located there."

"You're correct, and I could probably tell you a dozen more. But I believe mine will bring a special unique taste that this city has not yet had," he said, very confidently.

"What will make your restaurant any different from the others, Mr. Mariano?" Joyce asked.

"The difference is the authenticity. The Italian restaurants I've tried in this city are atrocious, compared to the real thing in Italy. I know what real Italian food should taste like. I was born and raised in Italy, and it's funny how people here try to imitate what we have been doing for centuries."

"Well, if you are a hundred percent sure this is what you want to do," she looked at him and smiled, "you have my services. Now, I have printed out a copy of the contract we've discussed, and left it with my secretary, so that you may get a chance to go over it before we make our final decision. Take some time to read it through, view my prices and fees, and have your attorneys to look it over. Do understand we are capable of getting the job done, and done well."

"Ms. Nickerson, I am very confident you can do this job and do it well. Otherwise, you would have never received a second thought. I trust my resource that referred you to me and I'm sure I will be greatly satisfied with your work. I have seen some already and checked out the current ones that are now on way. A pretty amazing job, I might say. For a woman in the construction business, you do superb work."

Deciding not to take his last comment as an insult, she smiled at him. "Well, thank you, Mr. Mariano." She signified the end of the meeting by standing up and extending her hand. "If that is all, I will be expecting a call from you not too many days from now, with any addendums you may have. Please do not forget to pick up your copy from the secretary out front."

He stood up reluctantly. "Yes, ma'am. I will let you know if anything needs to be negotiated. It's a pleasure to have your acquaintance, Ms. Nickerson." He reached over her desk to shake her extended hand.

"The same here, Mr. Mariano," she said, while walking around her desk to escort him out.

"Maybe when the time is right, you will grace me with your presence over dinner... let's say sometime this week," Mr. Mariano asked without moving from his spot.

Oh, God. Here we go. "I do not have private dinners with clients, Mr. Mariano, but thank you."

"Well, if not a private dinner, how about business... to discuss the addendums to the contract," he responded with a smile.

"In that case, as soon as you get back with me, we can discuss a date and time."

"Sounds good. Nice meeting you and see you soon."

Mr. Mariano left and Joyce sat down to review his file. This would be Mr. Mariano's first business and she wanted to make sure he knew what he was getting into. *Hmm, I thought the man was asking me on a date*, she shook her head. *Girl, you are something else. This man is very intelligent and very attractive.* She shook her head again, *this is work, Joyce. He's a client.* She moved his file over and picked up another client's file. She sat at her desk for five hours reviewing files, correcting contracts, and making blueprints before she realized she was hungry.

"Ms. Ruby," Joyce buzzed her secretary.

"Yes, Ms. Nickerson," Ms. Ruby answered.

"Could you please order my usual for lunch? I didn't realize how late it was."

"Yes, ma'am. That's the grilled chicken house salad with balsamic vinaigrette dressing, correct?"

"Yes, ma'am, with extra dressing, please. Thank you so very much."

"You're welcome. By the way, you have a phone call on line one." Ms. Ruby hung up before Joyce had a chance to ask who.

"Ms. Nickerson. How can I help you?" Joyce answered line one.

"Hey, Stranger," a deep voice greeted.

Joyce face broke out into a smile, and she rested her head against her chair. "Clint! It's been a few weeks. Where have you been?"

"Working. Have you had lunch yet?"

"Well, I just had Ms. Ruby order me something. Why? You miss me?" *I only wish.*

"You only wish," he chuckled. "How about meeting me for dinner tonight?"

"Why?" She turned her chair around to look out the window. The view was not of the sparkling ocean she once fantasized about, but of other tall buildings in different sizes, and a clear view of the sky. Lately, she's found herself wondering about what was on the other side of the fluffy white clouds. As a kid, she remembered stories of heaven and angels flying around with wings... as an adult, she wondered whether all of that was really true.

"Just thought maybe you'll want to hang out and finally try that new restaurant downtown we keep talking about."

"Yeah. Sure. What time?"

"Seven thirty. You'll probably be leaving the office around that time anyway, right."

Said more like a statement than a question, Joyce chuckled at the sarcasm in his voice. "Seven thirty sounds great. Plus, there's a question I've been meaning to ask you."

"Yeah? What is it?"

"I'll ask you tonight. I have to get back to work," she said, turning her view back to her computer. "See you later."

"Later." Clint hung up and Joyce went back to reviewing files and correcting contracts, not understanding her question would change her life forever.

✳ ✳ ✳

Joyce parked her car in the full parking lot of Bahama Jazz Cuisine, searching for Clint's car. *Lord, let him already have a table.* She picked up her cell phone and dialed his number.

"Hello," Clint answered with jazz music playing softly in the background.

"Hey. Are you here yet?"

"Yeah. I'm inside, seated. Once you come in, I'm four tables to your right."

"Great." She parked her car and walked into the brightly lit restaurant.

The smell of spicy meat and sweet fruits permeated the air, as the sound of Jamaican jazz music played softly in the background. Soft conversations buzzed in Joyce's ears from nearby tables as she made her way towards Clint. He smiled when he saw her, and she returned it. Giving him a brief kiss on the cheek when she reached the table, she sat on the seat across from him and immediately picked up the menu.

"I am famished. That salad I had for lunch did nothing for me."

Clint chuckled and took a sip of his water, "You're always hungry. I just don't know where all that food goes."

"Whatever." She glanced at the menu, seeing multiple things she would love to try. "Gosh, I shouldn't have come here on an empty stomach. Everything looks good."

"Well, choose one. How was work?"

"Long. You?"

"Same." He started to say something else when the waitress walked up.

"Good evening. My name is Roxie, and I'll be your server this evening. What can I get you guys to drink?"

"I'll have the kiwi tea and a glass of water," Joyce answered.

"And I'll have the strawberry lime fizz," Clint said.

"OK. That's the kiwi tea for the lady and strawberry lime fizz for the man. Are you ready to order or do you need a few minutes?"

Clint responded after giving Joyce a questionable look. "Are you ready, Joyce?'

"You go ahead, and by the time you're done I should be ready."

Clint ordered the jerk chicken breast, with a side of yucca, and mango rice. Joyce finally decided on fried goat, with sweet plantains, yucca, and a side salad, making up in her mind to come back later this week for the curry catfish. The waitress took their orders and came back five minutes later with their drinks. They sat in companionable silence, listening to the soft jazz playing in the background before Clint started the conversation.

"So... you said you had something to ask me. What was it?" Clint asked.

Joyce hesitated and stared at her glass of tea before responding. "How long have you been saved, Clint?"

"Well, almost all my life, but I got real serious about it when I got to college. I would say fifteen years."

"And you had no problems throughout the entire time? I mean... is it hard living saved? Being a Christian?"

"Oh, I had some problems, and living a Christian life was only hard when I didn't want to live it. Once I decided to get serious about my relationship with God, my lifestyle, my habits, my mind fell into place."

She looked at him confused. "I don't understand what you mean by 'once you got serious about it'. You told me before you were raised in the church and involved in so many things... how is that not being serious?"

Clint wasn't sure what brought all the questions, but he was definitely trying to contain himself from showing his excitement. He cleared his throat and took a sip of water, trying to gauge where this was going.

"Well, one can get busy with doing busy work in the church because of knowing what to do, but have no emotions or feelings behind it. I grew up in church, yes. I went to Great to Wait and talked about staying pure until marriage, I sung in the youth choir, did the step team... all of that was done because that's how I was raised. I had no choice but to do it. I enjoyed it because I had friends doing it right along with me, but all of that wasn't done because I loved God. It was done because I was told to and raised to."

He paused for a moment to see if she had any questions, then continued. "Once I got to college, I realized I had to make the decision to pray, read my word, and go to church for myself. I was on my own, no parents to bother me and watch my every move, no one to know what time I came home at night. Then one weekend, my parents came into town, so of course I went to church that Sunday. That's the Sunday God decided to play my childhood back to me." Clint's mind drifted to fifteen years ago.

Dressed in a white pressed shirt, navy blue jeans and black Calvin Klein Mully shoes, he sat in between his parents listening intently to what the pastor was saying. He couldn't explain what he was feeling at that time, all he knew was his heart felt overwhelmed and heavy. All of a sudden he saw himself at age seven crossing the street on his bike, not really paying attention to traffic, and a car swerving just in time to knick him off the bike. He got up scared but with no injuries. He saw himself at fifteen in a car with his cousins, when the driver fell asleep and hit the car in front of them, causing a domino effect with three other vehicles. He came out with a slight headache but no concussion. Many more scenes passed before him, then he heard a soft whisper, *all that I did was for you, not because your mother asked me to. I kept you because I love you.*

That Sunday he made up his mind to pursue a committed relationship with God. He shared this with Joyce, not noticing the effect until after he was done. He looked at her and was surprised at the bright glistening of her eyes.

Joyce quickly swiped at the tears and stared at her glass of water, deep in thought. They sat quiet for a few seconds, then she softly whispered, "That's what I want. For God to be so real to me the way He is to you."

"You can have that, Joyce. God is as real as... me sitting here in front of you."

"But..." Her voice caught and she cleared it. "But, how do I get there? How do I believe Him to be just that real?"

Clint reached across the table to grab her hand. "Just believe. It really is as simple as that. Believe that He's God... believe that He's real... believe that Jesus really died for your sins, and I promise you He will do the rest. He will show himself to you."

Clint knew this was the pivotal point for Joyce. He felt the struggle in her mind, and prayed that her need for God would win over the fear of being disappointed. They sat like this until the waitress returned. She quietly placed their foods in front of them, feeling this was an intimate time for the two, and walked away without disturbing them. For some reason she knew something entirely different was going on. She looked back at the couple, noticed the look on Joyce's face, and said a quick prayer, *Lord, help her see you for who you really are*, before moving to another table.

Joyce felt something light brush across her shoulders and her muscles loosened up. It then became clear to her what she had to do. She looked up, smiled at Clint, and squeezed his hand before letting go. She took a deep breath and picked up her fork. "Well... I guess it's safe to say I'll be joining you at church this Sunday." She chuckled at Clint's surprised look. "And don't say, 'about time'."

Clint laughed and picked up his fork. "About time."

chapter 14

I'NETA STEPPED OUTSIDE her home to throw the trash out, not realizing until she closed her door that Mason was sitting on top of his car across the street of her house. She froze in place not knowing what to do. She came up with many scenarios of what she would do if Mason finally showed himself, and now neither one of them came to mind. Not even when he started to approach her. She watched him with unsure eyes and still wasn't able to move as he stood before her.

"Hello, I'neta," Mason said when he stood a few feet away from her.

"You're not supposed to be here, Mason. The restraining order—," I'neta began to say.

"Is just a piece of paper that holds no power over me," Mason interrupted and finished. "I just want to talk to you. Just for a few minutes. We can sit on your porch where all your neighbors can see." He said while sitting on the bottom step. "I'm not here to beg or ask for another chance. I just want to talk to you."

I'neta couldn't read his expression, so she stood frozen in place, contemplating running back inside.

"I'neta, I'm the same guy you met and fell in love with almost a year ago."

"And the same guy who hit me," I'neta said, taking a step back.

Regret flashed in his eyes for a brief moment before he sighed and gave her a knowing smile. "I've apologized for that. And before you decide to make a run for it, think about the last time you ran for the door and didn't quite make it."

He watched the play of emotions on her face from the vicious memory of him slapping her, then patted the seat next to him. "Just one minute."

She thought about it and figured if he tried anything, her neighbors, especially Mrs. Young, had the police department on speed dial. She placed the trash between them and sat in a way she could run if he tried to grab her.

"The night I came here, I wasn't planning on hurting you," Mason began.

"You had a gun, Mason."

"Let me finish. That night I was dealing with some things I haven't told you about. Some personal things," Mason exhaled a shaky breath. "As a kid my mother used to beat me... a lot. I was an unplanned pregnancy, and she'd remind me every time she'd hit me. I was six when the beatings started, or when I actually realized she hated me," he said.

"Every night it was one thing or another. I left my shoe in the living room; I played too loud in my room; I had the audacity to breathe. Whatever reason she could find to beat me, she would. And if she couldn't find a reason, she'd beat me for the things I did that she didn't know about. It started off with her fist and as I got older she graduated to shoes, brooms... whatever she could get her hands on."

"Oh, my God." Joyce couldn't believe what she was hearing. In sympathy, she wanted to reach out to him, but history wouldn't let her.

"My father tried to stop her at first, but she'd jump on him." He looked at I'neta. "He wasn't much of a man. After a while, he'd just act like he didn't see it, or he'd leave the house and come back home hours later drunk." Mason sighed before he continued. "Every time she'd hit me, she would tell me she hated me. I slept on a mallet on the floor in our basement. And food... please. Only if she was having a good day would I have the chance to eat whatever was left over from her meal. My father finally left her, but that only made things worst. That night, to keep her from beating me, I stabbed myself with an old rusty screwdriver," he said with a smirk. "She didn't even take me to the hospital. Just poured some alcohol on it and covered it with a band-aid. It got infected and the school nurse had to dress it up."

"Wow, Mason. I am so sorry you had to go through that," I'neta said in amazement.

"You'll never know the half of it. It lasted for maybe three years before one of my teachers finally stepped in and called Family Services. They picked me up from school, took me to a foster home, and I haven't seen my mother since," he chanced another look at I'neta. "That night my whole childhood came back to haunt me. I couldn't take that agony anymore, so..." he shrugged. "Ending my life seemed right at that time." Not being able to stand the pity he saw in her eyes, he looked away. "I came here to apologize, then kill myself. I would rather be dead than let my mother exist in me."

"Mason, you are not your mother."

"I was becoming like her. I hurt someone I loved and didn't think twice about it. I knew I wasn't going to stop because it made me feel good. I felt like I finally had control over something."

He leaned against the stair and crossed his arms. "I don't want to be that kind of person, I'neta."

"At least you're able to admit how you felt and knew what it was. It takes a real strong person, Mason, to admit they were wrong, admit why they were wrong, and to want to change. You're stronger than your mother or father ever was. Yes, you came from them, but you don't have to be them. You choose where your future goes, Mason. Not them."

He turned to stare at her in amazement. "You are some-thing else. After what I've done to you, you can still sit here and see good in me. You really are an amazing woman."

"Thank you," she said, standing up. "I'm sorry for what your parents put you through, Mason. I wouldn't want to wish that on my worst enemy. But—"

Mason stood up also. "I didn't come here to convince you to take me back. I just wanted you to know."

"Thank you for letting me know, Mason." She stood in front of him not knowing what to say next. She decided there was nothing else to say and was about to tell him just that when she heard a distant sound of sirens. "Mason, why don't you just turn yourself in and stop running? How long do you think it'll take before they catch you? It'd be better this way."

"Well, if they want me they'll have to catch me. I'm gonna make them work for their salary." He took a step closer to I'neta with the intention of giving her a last hug, but changed his mind when he saw her flinched.

"I do thank you for listening to me, I'neta. I know I have no chance today, but some day I will be back." He smiled and ran his finger down her cheek. "You will always be mine. Remember that." He brushed his thumb across her lips before running back to his car and speeding off.

A few seconds later two squad cars sped by and a dark grey Chrysler stopped in front of her house. Joseph jumped out of the car with worry on his face. He pulled out his gun from its holster, ran into the house without saying anything to I'neta. She stood there holding the trash bag, waiting for him to come back out. He came out a few minutes later, securing his gun back into the holster.

"Are you okay," he asked I'neta, looking for visual signs of trauma.

"Yes, Joseph. I'm fine. A little shaken, but fine." She smiled at him, loving the care and worry in his eyes.

Stepping closer, he touched her face not believing she was okay. "He didn't hurt you, did he?" he asked as he stared into her eyes for any signs that she was lying.

"No. We just talked," she said, switching the bag from one hand to the other, she turned away from Joseph placing it into the garbage can.

"What do you mean, 'just talked'?"

"Just what I said, Joseph. We just talked." She walked passed him to get inside the house. "Are you coming in or are you going to keep standing out here gawking at the air?" I'neta asked.

Joseph followed her in and shut the door. She went into the kitchen to wash her hands, then took a seat on her couch. Joseph, on the other hand, did not bother sitting. He stared at her for a long time before he spoke.

"You do know this man is a fugitive, right?" Joseph asked.

"Yes, I do know that, Joseph." She sweetly smiled at him and patted the cushion next to her.

Ignoring the invitation, he crossed his arm and gave her a look of interrogation. "Yet, you didn't call the cops when he showed up?"

"Joseph, I didn't even know Mason was here until I stepped outside. By the time I got over my shock, he was standing in front of me. There was no running or cop calling I could have done at that moment. He said he wanted to talk, and that's what we did. It only lasted for maybe a few minutes."

"Do you know it's a crime to help and aid a fugitive, Ms. Villanucci?"

"Don't get formal with me, Joseph. And I was not, am not, aiding a fugitive. This has been the first time I've seen Mason since he'd escaped." She stood up, feeling herself getting irritated.

"I walked outside to throw my trash away. There was no reason for me to predict he was going to be out there. So, if you're implying something that I know I'm not going to like, you can get out of my house." She said, while walking to her door and flinging it open.

"I'm just doing my job, I'neta. I have to make sure…"

"Yeah, I know," I'neta said. She shut her door and walked to her kitchen. "Would you like something to drink?"

"Um… I'll take a glass of water, thank you." He finally took a seat on her couch and watched her in the kitchen. *She really is a beautiful woman. Why is it always the beautiful ones that have low self-esteem*, Joseph wondered. She came back with a glass of ice cold water, set it on top of a coaster on the coffee table in front of him, and sat next to him.

"I take it you're still here because you need a statement from me?" I'neta asked him.

"Well, I do, but that's not why I'm here. Actually, I've been off the clock since three. I was headed home when the call came in. I couldn't just keep on riding." He looked at her and wanted so badly to hold her. "Were you afraid?" he asked.

"No, just a little shaken. I kinda knew he wasn't going to hurt me. It was in his eyes, you know. Like... before, when he used to hit me, his eyes would change... to something ugly. But today when I saw him, he didn't have that glossy stare. I don't know how to explain it, but I knew he wasn't going to hurt me."

"What did you two talked about?" Joseph asked, using his expertise as a police officer to get more information about how she felt about this man.

"He wanted to explain to me why he came here the night he was arrested. You responding as quickly as you did saved both his life and mine." She glanced at Joseph before staring at her hands. "He also said I will always be his, and he'll be back."

Misunderstanding her expression to be that of interest, he asked, "Do you still have feelings for him, I'neta?"

Are we still on that, she asked herself. "No, I do not, Joseph. I know when to call it quits, and when something is unhealthy for me. I just know this guy, and I know how persistent he is."

"I only asked because..." *Joe, let it go*, he told himself. "Never mind. Look... I was planning on cooking dinner tonight and was hoping you would join me."

Accepting the topic change, she asked, "Where... at your place?" feeling a little uncomfortable.

"If that makes you too uncomfortable, maybe we can eat out somewhere." But seeing the expression on her face made him want to change his mind. "Unless you've already eaten."

"No, no. I just got off work myself and usually Mondays are crazy, so I haven't thought about what I wanted to eat. I do know I don't feel much like going out."

"Well, I guess that makes it a 'no'," Joseph said. "Or... maybe we can head to the grocery store and cook something here together." *I'm pulling at straws here.*

"I think I like that idea better," she smiled at him. "Can we leave now?"

"Now sounds great."

"Wait!" She remembered something. "I'm supposed to be mad at you."

"Well, obviously it wasn't that important," he responded, standing and bringing her up with him. "Are we taking my car or yours?"

"We'll take mine. We don't need another incident like the one we had the last time we were together." She grabbed her keys and purse off the counter and preceded him out. Dinner tonight was going to be something unusual for her.

❋ ❋ ❋

"OK... what do you feel like tonight?" Joseph asked I'neta as they strolled down the meat section. "Chicken, turkey, meatloaf, pork, seafood?"

"I don't know. I don't eat pork, though. Not for religious purposes, I just choose not to. And I try to stay away from red meat to keep my cholesterol low."

"Well, do you feel like something light or... I mean, give me a clue here."

"Hmm. What about breakfast? I think I can eat an omelet, with some turkey bacon, and maybe some grits or bowl of fruits."

Joseph turned to give her a weird look. "Breakfast for dinner?" He gave her a smile from ear to ear. "My kinda girl. I make a mean omelet. All we need is some diced tomatoes, onions, green peppers, eggs, etcetera etcetera."

"You can make mine without the onion. I can't stand 'em," she said, strolling after him as he made his way to the vegetable aisle. "But I would like to have pieces of bacon in my omelet, if you don't mind."

"No problem," Joseph said. They strolled down every aisle just to make time fly by. All they had to show for the hour at the grocery store were six items. They stood in line talking about nothing in particular, when the woman standing in front of them turned around quickly.

"Well, hello Joseph," the woman said. "I knew that was your voice I was listening to."

I'neta glanced at the woman and felt a pang of jealousy she quickly hid. The woman looked like she weighed one hundred pounds soak and wet, but wore her weight well. She stood close to Joseph's height and looked like she graced the runway for a living. Her eyes glistened with desire when she looked at him, until she saw I'neta.

"Hello, Amanda," he leaned forward to give her a hug, which was more of a pat on the back. "It's weird seeing you here."

"I'm sure it is, seeing that you never called me back."

Joseph cleared his throat and scratched his head. "I know. I'm sorry about that."

"I'm sure." She gave I'neta a once over and snickered.

Joseph turned to look at I'neta. "Amanda, this is I'neta. I'neta, Amanda."

I'neta reached over to shake her hand. "Hi."

"Hi." Amanda shook I'neta's fingers instead of her hand, and quickly dropped it. "I guess this explains why I haven't heard from you. I thought we were doing pretty good, if you ask me."

"Look, Amanda. I am sorry I didn't call you back. I should have told you I wasn't interested in dating anyone, but—"

"Funny how quickly things change," Amanda said, giving I'neta another look. "Hmm… he's cooking you dinner, too?" She glanced into the buggy and gave a sultry laugh. "What? No steak for her, Joseph? You chose her over me, but I got steak and she gets eggs." She laughed again, then turned to swipe her card.

I'neta held her tongue and swallowed the bitter taste in her mouth. She would never be caught in a cat fight with another woman over a man, but she really wanted to snatch the curly weave from this woman's head. When Amanda turned back around, I'neta gave her a sweet smile not giving her the satisfaction of seeing how upset she made her.

"Well, Joseph, it was definitely good seeing you. Don't be a stranger." She grabbed her bags and sashayed away, after blowing him a kiss and a wink.

I'neta rolled her eyes at her forwardness, while Joseph paid for the groceries. She made no attempt at conversation on the ride home, and ignored the small talk he tried to conjure up. She didn't want to compare herself to that woman, but she couldn't ignore how gorgeous she was. *Am I able to even compete with her?* She sighed in resignation, keeping her focus on the road.

With a shake of his head, he exhaled and cleared his throat. "I'm sorry about that. She was the woman I told you I was dating a few months ago."

"I kind of figure that out. Seems like she took it pretty hard." She stared straight ahead, not daring to look at him for this question. "You didn't... um.... you know." She looked at him awkwardly. "I mean... for a woman to be a little upset about not being called, it usually means something more happened and she feels... you know... kind of used."

"Are you asking whether I slept with her?" Joseph asked.

"Yes, I am."

"No, we did not sleep together. The woman was kind of... how do I put it...," he sighed. "She was a little too clingy too early. On our first date, she was making wedding plans... literally. She said by next year this time she would like to be planning our wedding or getting married. That was a little too much for me. Plus, she's not the kind of woman I'm looking for," Joseph spoke honestly.

"So, what kind of woman are you looking for? What sparks your interest?" I'neta asked.

"Well, she has to be a Christian, first. Some men don't too much make that a requirement, but the Bible says 'Can two walk together, unless they are agreed?' There is no way I can start a healthy relationship with a woman if she doesn't have God in her life. That's just asking for trouble. Secondly, I usually find women that rarely say anything about themselves interesting to me. You know, this is Miami, so everywhere you turn, some woman is talking about how good she looks or how much she makes. A woman who asks more questions about you than giving information about herself sticks out to me. I don't know... maybe it's the cop in me. I usually see what others don't."

"What do you see when you look at me?" I'neta asked, curious of what he saw when he looked at her.

"I see a lot when I look at you," he responded, seeing how tight she grasped the steering wheel. *She's getting nervous again*, he observed. "I see a beautiful woman, with a big wall she's built to keep others out because of what some man did to her. I see this aggressive stance you try to hold because of having to always fight for the things you want. I see a little bitterness you have towards your mother..." He stopped there, thinking he'd said too much.

"What did you say?" she said, glancing at him.

"You hold a little bitterness towards your mom," he repeated. *No need to back down now, she already heard.*

"I've never said anything about my mother to you, so you don't know how I feel about her," she said angrily. "I love my mother."

But she blames her for what happened as a child.

"I know you do, but you blame her for what happened to you when you were younger." He knew he had to stop when she braked hard, trying to keep from hitting a truck. She didn't say anything else, and neither did he, until she parked her car in front of her home.

"What happened to me as a girl, Joseph? What do you know?" I'neta asked him after turning the ignition off and facing him.

"I don't know anything. All I know is... that's what I see when I look at you. You have this wall and it's not because of what this man did to you. It goes deeper. And... I've been with you for over an hour and you didn't pick up the phone to call your mother once to tell her what happened. Almost every woman I know that has a mom calls her to tell everything."

"Well, I'm not like every woman, Joseph," she said, opening her door. "And if I find out you've been snooping around trying to get information on me, this friendship is over... before it even starts." She emphasized it with slamming her car door.

See, Lord. You gave me this prophetic gift and all it does is get me into trouble... sometimes. How am I supposed to woo her if she is constantly getting mad at me, Joseph prayed.

Joseph sat in the car for a little while before going into the house. She left the door unlocked, so he guessed he could still come in. Once he stepped in, he saw her in her kitchen rinsing off the utensils needed to make dinner. He placed the bag of groceries down on the kitchen counter and handed her the vegetables to rinse off. She did and made sure he had everything he needed, all without saying a word, before walking out of the kitchen to turn the television on. She flipped through channels before landing on the History Channel, then threw the remote control down.

"Couldn't find anything to watch?" Joseph asked, in means to strike up a conversation.

"Ridiculous. I don't know why I'm paying for this dish if I can't get a good movie to watch," she said.

"Pop a DVD in. One of your favorites. Let's see what kind of taste you have in movies."

"All right, but I warn you. I'm not an ordinary girl. My movie taste may be totally different than a lot of people," she said, looking through her stand of DVDs. She finally chose one after ten minutes of indecisiveness. She popped it in and waited for the previews to bypass before hearing what Joseph had to say once he realized what movie they were about to watch.

"Well, well, well. 'Ice Age' huh. There's nothing unordinary about watching animated movies. There are a lot of people who do."

"Joyce always gives me trouble about watching these things and cartoons. I can't help it. I love 'em."

"That's because Joyce has never been a child so she doesn't appreciate the simple things, like cartoons and... 'Ice Age'. As a matter of fact, this is one of my favorite movies. Turn up the volume." Joseph continued making their breakfast-dinner, all being entertained by the pure enjoyment on I'neta's face. She laughed at some parts, got teary-eyed in one, all like this was her first time seeing this. Her dining table was already prepared, so all he had to do was place the food and their drinks on the table. Without being called, she turned the movie off, washed her hands, and sat down on at the table.

"Mmm, smells pretty good. I hope it taste the same," I'neta complimented. She grabbed her fork and was about to dig in when Joseph gently grasped her hand.

"Let's bless the food before we enjoy it."

"Oh, yes..." She placed her fork beside her plate. "I'm sorry about that." She bowed her head and reached across the table to grasp Joseph's other hand.

Ignoring the shock that ran through his body at her mere gentle touch, Joseph bowed his head and blessed the food. "Father, we thank you for this time that we both can come together and enjoy a meal. We ask that you bless the food and allow it to add the appropriate nutrients we need. Thank you for providing the finances that provided this meal. It's in your name we pray."

"Amen," they both said in unison. She took a bite of the omelet and thanked God that this man knew how to cook. *Maybe he is a pretty good catch. He's handsome, protective, and has a job. So far he's been respectful, minus the two small incidents... and kind. A little too kind if you ask me... for a man, at least. I wonder what he's hiding.* She looked up from her plate, and watched him eat silently. "So, Joseph, how many women have you dated?"

"Well, I've dated a few but only became serious with two. And when I say serious, I mean we actually had a relationship."

"What happened with those two?" I'neta asked in mere curiosity.

"Well, the first girl was during high school. We dated for five years, from ninth grade to sophomore year in college, but once we moved here from Chicago she decided she wanted to see other people. We broke up and she moved back home after a year of school. I believe she's married now with two daughters, and pastoring." Joseph looked at her and placed a forkful of omelet in his mouth.

"Did it bother you that she married someone else? I mean, I'm sure you thought this was the woman you were supposed to be with forever?" I'neta asked.

He swallowed before responding. "When we first broke up, yes, I was hurt, but by the time she got married I was well over it." He drunk some water, then continued. "I was happy her husband found her. She and I were put into each other's lives for just a season and that season was over once we came to college. I learned a lot from that relationship and that's what I believe God intended for us to do when we got together... learn certain things about the opposite sex, strengthen each other, show what love really is. Yeah, we were young, but we did love each other genuinely."

"So, what about the second woman you were in relationship with? How did that end?" I'neta asked while taking a sip of her orange juice.

Joseph sighed before beginning the story. "Well, the second woman I fell in love with was a co-worker. We started off being friends and there were no intentions, on my part, to start a relationship. I knew and she knew there was no way she and I could be together because of our different lifestyles."

"You going to church and her not?"

"Precisely. Well, after a while of hanging out, we developed feelings for each other. The next thing I know, we're in a relationship and getting intimate." He looked at I'neta. "Too intimate. Things got out of control and that's because I chose to be disobedient to God when He told me not to start a relationship with this woman. That lasted for about two years before I finally listened to God and ended the relationship. It was very hard to let her go, and I think that was because I allowed myself to become attached to her in more ways than one. Since then, I haven't really dated anyone, except for that one I had a few months ago. I've been single for about eight years now."

"Wow. I don't know what to say. Seems like a lot of you church goers make more mistakes than us folks who aren't." She took another bite of her food in an attempt to avoid his eyes. "I use to date a minister," she said, exhaling loudly.

Here goes nothing, she says to herself before telling him. "During my freshman year I had a classmate who was always inviting me to church. Finally, one day I went and loved it. I became a frequent visitor and finally joined when I made up my mind to live right. I got saved, stopped the drinking, the clubbing, all that other mess that comes along with loving this world. Well, he was a very young man and very much handsome and single, but I wasn't interested in him or getting into a relationship. While most girls were all over him, I went the opposite direction. Tried my best to not linger around and catch his attention, but I guess my actions drew more attention from him than I wanted."

She looked up at Joseph. "He started to pursue me; wanted a relationship, took me out to eat... dancing... poetry readings... the whole nine yards. Then his whole attitude changed. He started rubbing on me more, kissing me, coming over late at night. At first, I was a little uncomfortable and I told him so. He said he was falling in love with me and didn't know how to contain it. Late nights led to him spending the night... and spending nights led to us sleeping together. I started feeling used and just plain ol' wrong. When I spoke to him about it, he covered it up by saying we were going to get married anyway, so God will forgive us."

Here comes the hard part. I can't believe I'm telling him this. "Then one day I went for my regular yearly checkup. Doctor told me I was pregnant. Timothy 'bout had a cow. He told me to have an abortion." She shrugged off the tense feeling that usually rode up her shoulders when she thinks about this.

"My God!" Joseph said.

"My sentiments exactly. At first I argued with him and told him I couldn't do that." A tear started to roll down her face. "That was the first time he slapped me. I was so shocked I didn't get a chance to defend myself. He slapped me a few more times, then walked out ending the relationship. I decided I didn't want a piece of him in my life forever... so I got rid of it." Now, full-grown tears were rolling down her face. "That was the worst experience of my life."

"And that's when you gave up on God," Joseph said.

"Somethin' like that. I didn't go back to church, but the word on the street was he confessed his sins to the congregation. Told them he allowed himself to get wrapped up with a whore, was tempted and fell to temptation. He told them I got pregnant by another man and tried to put it on him. Worst part… they believed him." She didn't know what else to do but to keep crying.

I'neta prided herself on not crying in front of men, but she just couldn't stop. She never cried about the baby, about Timothy, about what the church folks said, and all that seemed to be coming out now. For a while all she heard was her weeping voice, then she suddenly felt strong arms engulf her and heard a strong masculine voice in her ear… praying.

"Help her to see that every bad she has ever encountered in her life, you have used for her good and will continue to do so, God. Erase the hurt, the pain, the disappointments, and help her to forgive this man that has done her wrong. Most importantly, Father, help her to forgive herself. I thank you, God, for deliverance in her life. I thank you for healing, salvation, and love that surpass all understanding."

Tell her that I love her.

"I'neta, God loves you so much and desires to make you His. He says you will never understand the depth of His love for you, but it's not for you to understand, it's for you to have. He says everything you ever worried about, everything that ever troubled you, He has them. Just let it go so He can do what He pleases with them. He doesn't want you to have to worry about one thing. He says your past will never push Him away, because it's the past. When He looks at you, He sees a beautiful woman He made in His image. A woman He made just to please Him. A woman who is capable of touching His heart like no one else does. He says, He's the missing puzzle piece in your life, and He wants so badly to commune with you, but He will not force Himself on you. He is too much of a gentleman for that. You have to say yes, I'neta. Yes, to all the promises He has for you. Yes, to whatever He has planned for your life. Yes to forgiveness, to His peace, love, joy, all that comes with having a relationship with God. You, I'neta, have to say yes."

I'neta did not remember how she ended up on the floor, but she was with Joseph's arms around her and God's voice in her ear. She cried long and hard, then finally let everything go and told God 'yes'.

chapter 15

In a nervous gesture, Joyce brushed an unseen lint off her navy blue tailored skirt for the umpteenth time. Standing beside her car, she looked up at the tall, red brick building not sure what to expect. Butterflies danced in her stomach, while she mustered up the courage to move her feet. *What am I afraid of anyway? It's just church.* She looked to her left and noticed the parking attendant dancing a jig while directing a car, to her right a family of three walked passed her in a hurry. She exhaled, shook the nervousness off, and buttoned her navy blue blazer securely. *It's just church.*

Entering into the foyer of Changing Lives Ministry, Joyce admired the beautifully lit hall and the art work on display. Standing in front of the sanctuary door was a middle aged woman, who had no problem greeting Joyce with a warm hug. "Well, good morning. Welcome to Changing Lives. I'm Esther and you are?"

Taken aback by the sudden show of affection, it took Joyce a few seconds to answer. "Joyce... my name is Joyce. Please to meet you."

"The pleasure is mine, Dear. Is this your first time visiting with us?"

"Yes, ma'am, it is."

"Great!" She reached behind her to pull out a small gift bag from a beautifully crafted shelf and handed it to Joyce. "Here's a little gift to say thank you for joining us today. Inside you will find a visitor's card. If you would fill that out and give that to one of the ushers before leaving, that would be great."

"Yes, ma'am, I will. Thank you."

"Be blessed. And may God reveal Himself to you in a way He has never done before."

She smiled and nodded her head at the greeter, making her way inside the sanctuary. On each wall there was a banner hanging with names of God displayed in beautiful art form, the chandeliers were bright enough windows were not needed, and three columns of navy blue seats sectioned off the church. Light chatter permeated the room as Joyce scanned the area for a seat. She walked towards the column to her right, and found a seat on the fourth row next to a young woman with a sleeping toddler on her lap. She looked up as Joyce placed her purse on the seat between them, and gave a sincere smile.

"Good morning. Welcome to Changing Lives. I would give you a hug right now, but..." she nodded her head towards the baby and gave Joyce an apologetic smile." He's been fussy all morning, and I've just gotten him to sleep."

"Oh, that's fine. I'm Joyce by the way."

"Nice to meet you. I'm Shirley. Is this your first time here?"

"It is." Joyce said, and left it at that.

"Well, I pray you enjoy yourself. We're about to start in a few minutes."

Almost on cue the musicians started playing a soft melody while a group of six people graced the pulpit. Joyce scanned the church hoping to see Clint, but could not find him. A little nervous about not knowing anyone, she was hoping Clint would be the first person she ran into but knew it wasn't likely. He had already warned her he'll be teaching the Men Sunday School class that morning, and may run late getting upstairs. As the singers started singing a soft melody and other people ended their conversations to make it to their seats, Joyce made up in her mind that she'd be sitting alone until she felt a soft touch on her shoulder. She turned to see who it was and smiled at the familiar face of her friend.

Clint reached over to give her a hug. "Glad to finally see you here. Move over for me."

Joyce grabbed her purse and placed it under the seat in front of her as she moved over. "I thought I was going to have to catch up with you later."

"Now, I wouldn't do that to you." He looked at her again, and the look he gave Joyce made the butterflies return. "I am really glad you made it. Really glad." He squeezed her hand and gave her a sweet smile before turning to give his full attention to the singers.

Clint wasn't sure why, but when he walked into the sanctuary and saw Joyce his heart fluttered in his chest. Never an emotion he felt towards her before. When he looked into her eyes, he felt the flutter again and another emotion he couldn't quite put his finger on. For some reason she looked different to him, and being with her in this setting felt... perfect. He wanted to hold her in his arms but settled for squeezing her hands. He had to force himself to let go instead of holding it throughout the service. He sneaked another glance at her trying to figure out what was different about her, making him feel this way.

Joyce was unsure of how to dissect Clint's mood. The way he looked at her felt... strange. His tone was a little softer too. And when he squeezed her hand, he brushed his thumb across her knuckles causing weird sensations to run through her. *Maybe he's just happy you finally came to church after all these years of inviting you*, she chided. Regardless, being here with him felt... complete. She shook the emotion that was rising and focused her attention on the singers.

After praise and worship, there was a brief moment the members came around to greet all the visitors. Joyce found herself being hugged by so many people she didn't know, but did not feel violated. Right before sitting, she felt a slight tap on her shoulder and turned to give another person a hug.

Joyce slightly hesitated in surprise when seeing who the person was, but quickly recovered by wrapping her arms around her. "Eileen! How have you been?" Expecting to hear a sarcastic remark laced with bitterness, Joyce prepared herself for the attack.

"I'm good, Joyce. Very good." Eileen gave Joyce a genuine smile and winked her eyes at Clint. "I see he has finally persuaded you to come. It's really good to see you, Joyce. Hope to see you again."

Eileen gave Joyce another hug before walking away to hug another visitor. Joyce watched her walk away, not sure how to take it in. Months ago Eileen would have given Clint the third degree about having Joyce here, let alone sitting next to her. Joyce couldn't quite put her finger on it, but Eileen looked much better than she did months ago.

"She's changed a lot since our break up. Kind of matured some," Clint responded.

"Good for her. I was unsure how she was going to react..." Joyce was amazed of how much Eileen has changed. "Looks like getting rid of you was the best decision she could have made."

Chuckling, Clint elbowed Joyce on the side. Joyce returned the favor, feeling much more at ease. After the choir sang, the announcements played, and offering given, Clint's pastor- Pastor Manning- stood up to preach his sermon. Joyce wasn't sure what his topic was, but it stemmed from forgiveness. She was so intent on what he was saying, she forgot everyone else around her. She felt as if he was speaking to her directly and in desperation.

In the middle of his sermon, Pastor Manning picked up his Bible and walked from behind the podium to stand in front of the column Joyce was sitting. "For the Bible says in John 20:23, 'If you forgive the sins of any, they are forgiven them; if you retain the sins of any, they are retained.' You hold the power of forgiveness in your hands, but forgiveness is not just for the person who has hurt you. Forgiveness also frees you from them. Imagine this... in order to keep someone under the pressure of your unforgiveness, you have to hold them down. The only way to keep them there is by holding them down. You can't move forward, you can't walk, you can't even use your hands to eat because you have to make sure they stay under you. Not only do you keep them in bondage, but you keep yourself there. Forgiveness is for you also."

Walking back to stand behind the podium, Pastor Manning laid his Bible down then looked throughout the congregation. With so much sincerity in his voice he said, "For those of you struggling with forgiving someone, whether a parent, a significant other, yourself... maybe even God, you have to let that go."

Moving to stand in front of the podium he continued. "Now, for those of you thinking 'God doesn't need forgiveness. He cannot do any wrong', I totally agree. But some of us have blamed Him for things that have happened in our lives. We felt He could have prevented them, He could have protected us... do something so we wouldn't hurt. For those of you feeling that way, you have to forgive God in your hearts. Understand that everything He allowed to happen was just to build your character, and you will come out better in the end. If you can't understand that but really want to, I want you to come up here for prayer. If you want to finally use your power to forgive someone, then I want you to come up here for prayer. If you're tired of being bitter because of your past, I want you to come up here for prayer."

Every word Pastor Manning spoke seemed to pierce Joyce's heart. How did he know so much about her? She blamed Noel for what he did, she blamed herself for staying so long in the relationship, and she blamed God for allowing her child to die. She held that in her heart for so many years, she didn't know how to let it go. She didn't even know if she wanted to. Should she give Noel her forgiveness? Should she forgive herself for being dumb?

Yes... I deserve it and I need to. She answered the questions herself, allowing herself to join the group that was slowly growing at the altar. She felt someone stand next to her and heard a woman whisper in her ear, "Can I pray for you?" Joyce nodded without even looking to see who it was. It wasn't like she knew who everyone was anyway. She closed her eyes and told herself it was just her and God.

Pastor Manning came back on the mic. "Those of you at the altar repeat after me. Father..."

"Father, I know that my life is in your hands and you know all things. I ask that you'll forgive me for not forgiving those who have hurt me. Give me the power and the desire to forgive them, myself, and you." Joyce repeated every word with so much urgency, wanting and hoping God heard her heart. "Heal me from bitterness, from unforgiveness, from hatred. Create in me a clean heart and renew a right spirit within me."

"Now... in your own words, speak to God," Pastor Manning said.

God, I know I'm a sinner. But only you can erase my sins and allow me to start all over again. I do believe you are God and the son of God, and you came down from heaven to die for my sins. I do believe you raised yourself up from the dead and now I have the chance to live. Please, accept me as your child today. I ask you to come into my life and my heart.

Joyce felt the woman next to her engulfed her in her arms, and the need to cry overtook her. She felt something she had never felt in her life. The hurt she held in her heart, the fear, the disappointment, the anger were no longer heavy. She no longer felt she was an outsider looking in, but now fitted in this life of salvation.

"Now, open your mouth and thank God for what He's just done. Give Him praise for forgiveness." Pastor Manning led the congregation in praise.

Joyce did exactly that... thanked God for another chance at life.

✳ ✳ ✳

After service, Joyce spoke with Clint for a brief moment before declining lunch and heading home. Any other time she would have jumped at the chance of spending some time with him, but she didn't want to lose what she was feeling to what she felt for Clint. She wanted to enjoy this new love in her heart for God, and didn't want to cheat that with her confused emotions about Clint.

She opted to go home and spend some quality time by herself. Parking her car inside the garage, she remembered she hadn't checked her mail yesterday, and went to do exactly that. She flipped through a few bills and junk mail until she finally found the one addressed from Judge Athens. *Bingo. It's finally here.* She tore the envelope open, and it took her but a few minutes to realize what the letter was saying. *God, no. Not yet. I'm not ready.*

Joyce read the letter a few more times to make sure she was clear on what it said. So engulfed in what she was reading, she didn't hear the car pull up until I'neta slammed the car door.

"Hey, Girl. Just getting home?" I'neta asked, greeting Joyce with a kiss on her cheek.

"Yeah," she responded, still looking down at the letter. "Read this," Joyce handed the letter to I'neta and watched her face while she read.

I'neta read the letter twice before giving Joyce her full attention. "So, this means..."

"Yes, in a few months Noel should be out on parole." Joyce turned to walk inside. I'neta followed, throwing her keys down next to Joyce's on the table that stood near the door. Joyce took her blazer off and threw it on the couch, while walking to the kitchen to grab herself a bottle of water. "I got saved today," said Joyce, matter-of-factly.

"What?" I'neta stood still looking at her. "Well, bring your tail over here and give me a hug." I'neta ran to her and squeezed her as tight as she could. "Congratulations!"

"Well, I didn't think you'd be this excited." She returned the hug, sensing something was different about her friend. I'neta seemed... more pleasant.

"I didn't tell you because I wanted you to figure it out yourself, but I got saved a few nights ago. Joseph was there to guide me through it. It was just time, Joyce." I'neta pulled back to look at Joyce's face. "Oh, Friend. This is the most exciting news of my life. Both of us saved at the same time. Woohoo!" I'neta giggled like a six year old and danced a jig to the living room, all giddy and excited.

Joyce couldn't help but join in the laughter and the dance. "Congratulations to you, too, I'neta." She threw herself on the couch.

I'neta threw herself on the couch next to Joyce. "So, tell me how do you feel?"

"New. Like I can conquer the world. I know it sounds silly."

"Not at all. I know exactly what you mean. It feels great."

"It does. Since that accident months ago, I've been trying to decide whether I need to go ahead and give my life to God. I don't know why but I was scared to. Then, earlier this week I kind of felt like I had to. You know? Almost like, God was rushing me to do it."

"I know what you mean, Joyce. It was just time. Who knows? Maybe it's because Noel is about to be released."

Joyce shivered at the thought of the man who hurt her and caused her to lose her child being released from prison. "I can't believe after just five years they're going to let him out on parole! What if he comes looking for me? What if he hasn't changed and..." The fear in her eyes spoke volumes.

"First of all, Noel wouldn't dare put his hands on you because God will not allow it. He didn't allow you to survive all that abuse years ago to bring you here and allow him to hurt you again. Secondly, you're not the old Joyce you use to be. You've grown a back bone from somewhere and I've watched you handle your own in tough situations." She grabbed Joyce's face with both hands, forcing her to look at her. "You're not afraid of him anymore. There is nothing he can do to you. OK?

"OK." Joyce leaned in to hug her friend, glad she had someone as strong and supportive as I'neta on her side.

"I'm hungry. Let's go celebrate." I'neta jumped up.

"I don't know. I have to finalize some projects before the end of the week."

"Oh, leave work at work. Come on... my treat."

"In that case, I'm in. Where are we going?" Joyce asked.

"How about Shrimp Seas? My assistant, Angela, was telling me they serve a real good seafood salad," I'neta said. "I've wanted to try them for a while now."

"Sounds good to me."

Shrimp Seas was located in South Beach, so I'neta volunteered to drive her car. Passing by Bayside, Joyce thought about her first date with Edmund and smiled, wondering what was he up to these days. The last time she spoke to him a few weeks ago, he was seeing a young lady from his church.

They arrived at Shrimp Seas thirty minutes later to a full parking lot. I'neta drove around in circles for ten minutes before a parking space became available.

"I surely hope all these cars out here means the food is really good." I'neta parked and they both strolled into the restaurant, deciding to wait the twenty minutes for a table. As they were escorted to their table, both were engulfed in the ambience they didn't see a young man stand until I'neta nearly ran into him.

"Oh, excuse..." she looked up into familiar eyes and stepped back once she realized who it was. "me."

"Hello, I'neta. Joyce." Timothy barely gave Joyce a glance as he stared at I'neta. His eyes twinkled and his face distorted into a smirk.

I'neta nodded and attempted to walk pass him, but he blocked her path. "What, Timothy?" she asked.

"It's really good seeing you. I was hoping to talk and catch up." He looked toward his table and nodded at the empty seat in front of him. "Why don't you join me for a bit?"

"Why? Your girlfriend's running late?" I'neta smirked.

"She's hardly my girlfriend, and jealousy doesn't fit you well."

I'neta laughed and shook her head, attempting to bypass him again.

He stepped to the left, keeping her from passing by. "Oh, come on. Don't tell me you're still pining over what happened years ago. I thought you'll be over that by now." Lowering his voice to a whisper, he leaned a little closer to her ear, "It's not like we both could have handled a child at that time anyway. I did us both a favor by making you get rid of it."

I'neta glared at him with fire in her eyes and swiftly slapped him. The gasp from nearby tables didn't stop her from slapping him a second time. "You conniving, self centered, egotistical—"

Joyce grabbed I'neta's hand and quieted her from continuing. "I'neta, let's go. This fool doesn't deserve that much energy."

I'neta looked at him again and wanted to slap the smirk off his face, but decided to walk away. The rage she felt inside at the audacity of him was totally different than the love she once thought they shared. She remembered the afternoons they would walk on the beach, and the talks they would have late nights. He made her feel as if she was a precious gem, and the only woman he could ever love. The way he would lightly kiss her forehead after a date and gently squeeze her in a hug made her feel cherished. She had to admit… the expertise of a heartless womanizer fooled her good.

The waiter waited for them to sit before placing their napkins on their laps. He cleared his throat and bashfully looked at I'neta. "Are you okay ma'am?"

I'neta nodded, embarrassed to look at him. "I am. Thank you."

"OK. Well, my name is Andrew. What can I start you off to drink?"

Seeing I'neta struggling to get her composure, Joyce answered for the both of them. "We'll have a sweet tea, please."

"Sweet tea it is. I'll be back in a brief moment." The waiter quickly walked away as if his heels were on fire.

Joyce waited for I'neta to finish her breathing exercise before reaching over to grasp her hand. "Are you OK?"

"Yes." She finally was able to look at Joyce and slightly smiled. "Guess salvation doesn't get rid of all that anger and bitterness you hold inside?"

"I'm sure it does. Probably takes more time than we expect. I mean, what's the point of getting saved if it won't give us something different than what we're use to, right? All that we've been holding inside, you know… the nasty, ugly, repulsive things, have to leave sooner or later."

"Hopefully sooner than later," I'neta stated. She exhaled and shook her shoulders, then gave Joyce a wide grin. "That felt good, though."

"What?" Joyce asked as if she didn't know where this was headed.

"Slapping him. Gosh, it felt good to get that out." I'neta laughed and grabbed the menu.

Joyce laughed and shook her head, amazed at her friend. "I bet it did. But seriously… are you okay eating here?"

I'neta's head snapped up from the menu, eyes full of confusion. "Why wouldn't I be? Girl, Timothy does not have that much power over me." She placed the menu down and folded her hand. "It's just... what he said just... I never forgave myself for having that abortion. So, the anger from making that decision reared its ugly head." I'neta shrugged and picked up the menu again, hoping to drop the subject.

Joyce almost decided to leave the subject alone, and not respond to the guilt and bitterness in I'neta's voice but she couldn't leave it alone. After a few minutes of silence, and the waiter brought their drinks and took their orders, Joyce looked at her and decided to say it anyway.

"Look... you messed up a few years ago. Made a messed up decision. Lived with it for years and will probably live with it for more years. But, you have to stop beating yourself over this. It's done. There is nothing you can do to bring it back. And if what Clint has been telling me all these years about God forgiving us for our past mistakes, you have to start forgiving yourself too. What's the point of trying to start a new life if you're going to bring all the baggage from the past with it?" Joyce realized by the look on I'neta's face, what she was saying was hitting home. "We have to let go of those things holding us to our past, or I future won't be any different."

chapter 16

JOYCE SAT ON her office chair, gazing out the window with the phone to her ear. Her conversations with Clint had taken a weird but pleasant turn since attending church with him a few weeks ago. She wondered, for the umpteenth time, whether he was being this way because she finally got saved or was his feelings for her developing into something more. Could four years of suppressed affection finally be reciprocated? *Yeah right.* Twice she'd shown him how she felt, and both times he shot her down. How many times does one have to get let down? *Twice is my limit.* But for the past few weeks, Joyce had to turn down many invitations to accompany Clint somewhere, which brings her back to this conversation.

"I'm sorry, Clint, but I won't be able to make it to the movies tonight. I have a business dinner with Mr. Mariano in about two hours to discuss our contract."

"Since when have you gone on dates with business prospects?" Clint asked with a hint of jealousy in his tone. He couldn't believe Joyce was cancelling on him again. This made it five times within the last few weeks.

"It's not a date. It's business and I've been doing it for years. I have dinner or lunch with all of my business prospects, both male and female. And why do you sound jealous?" Joyce asked in surprise.

"I'm not jealous. Just wondering why you've cancelled on me every week for the past three."

"I've been swamped at work. It has nothing to do with you. It's just that business has been picking up, which means I have to spend more time at the office. We can go to the movies this Saturday." Joyce felt like she was speaking to a boyfriend rather than a friend. *I've never had to explain myself to Clint before.* "Are you feeling okay? Do you need me to stop by on the way home?"

"No. I'm good. Just be careful tonight, all right. Sometimes men can take something as minute as a business dinner and turn it to something that it's not."

Clint genuinely sounded worried, so Joyce decided to put his mind at ease. "I'm only meeting him for half an hour. So, more like drinks. We're just going to sign some papers, shake hands, and voila, I'm done. I'll even call you on the way home. How does that sound?"

"Woman, please. Just be careful." Clint ended the call hearing Joyce's soft giggle on the other end.

Joyce continued to work on other projects before preparing to meet Mr. Mariano at seven o'clock that evening. She was excited this project would be bringing in ten percent more than her usual contracts, which made her anxious to get his name signed on the line.

As she prepared for her meeting with Mr. Mariano, Ms. Ruby knocked on her door and stood at the entrance without saying a word. Joyce noticed the worried expression on her face and gave her full attention.

"What's the matter, Ms. Ruby?" Joyce asked as she placed documents inside her suitcase. She wanted to make sure everything was with her when she met Mr. Mariano at the restaurant.

"I wanted to know… would it be okay to accompany you tonight?"

Taken aback by the request, Joyce stopped midway into putting documents in her case. "Why?"

"Well, I've always been curious about how things work on your end, and thought maybe tonight would be a great night to shadow you." Ms. Ruby entered the office completely, and Joyce saw not just worry but panic in her eyes.

"What's really going on, Ms. Ruby?"

Ms. Ruby slid herself on the seat across from Joyce and fidgeted with her collar before actually saying what was on her mind. "I have a weird feeling about Mr. Mariano. Something about him doesn't seem right, and I hate the way he gawks at you."

"He does not gawk," Joyce began to argue.

"He stares as if he has plans to get inside your pants, and it disturbs me. I just don't think you should be meeting him alone tonight."

"Ms. Ruby, I truly appreciate your concern, but really, I will be okay. I'm only going to be there for thirty minutes so he can sign some papers, and I'm off home. I promise I'll be okay." Joyce loved how Ms. Ruby worried about her. She's been the closest thing to a mother these past few years.

Ms. Ruby knew once Joyce had it in her head she was going to do something, there was no stopping her. She tried one more suggestion before ending it.

"Why don't you have Clint join you both?"

Joyce went back to shuffling papers inside her suitcase. "Clint has plans to go to the movies tonight. I'm not going to bother him about a thirty minute meeting. Seriously, Ms. Ruby, I will be okay."

With that said she continued to check the last documents before sticking them into the suitcase. Ms. Ruby shook her head at Joyce's stubbornness, then left her office preparing to close up for the day.

❇ ❇ ❇

"Joseph?"

"Hmm?"

"I need to tell you something." I'neta and Joseph were watching a movie at her place. He was lying on the couch while she sat on the love seat. He was so engulfed into the movie that she didn't think he noticed her staring at him for an hour now, trying to figure out how she was going to say what she needed to tell him.

He sat up and placed the movie on pause. He knew she had a lot on her mind because she hardly watched the movie. He ignored the fact that she was staring at him and figured whatever she had to say would come in her timing. "I'm all ears," he said, giving her his full attention.

Just say it, she told herself. "As a child my mother dated a lot of men, before and after my father ended up in prison. He's been locked up since I was twelve and is still in there... for attempted murder." She exhaled, getting ready to tell him the whole ordeal.

"When I was twelve my mother had a real drug problem. She thought she hid it well, and for years she did, but things got more demanding when she lost her job and my father was the only one working. He wouldn't give her cash when she asked for it, knowing what she was going to spend it on. Instead, he would ask her what she wanted and got it for her. She got desperate and started selling herself for it." She looked across at Joseph to see if he was following along, and he nodded his head for her to continue.

"Men would come over to the house, she would take them to the back room and they would leave after half an hour, and she would be sniffing whatever it was they left. Luckily, I didn't see much because I'd be in school during the day. By the time I got home, one man would be leaving, and before five o'clock someone else would be coming in." Feeling like she was being constrained, she stood up and started pacing.

"I knew my father had to know because he would come home and they would start arguing. Anyways, one day I was home on a holiday break. It was just my mother and I... my father had to work. He asked me about three times that morning if I wanted to go to work with him and I said 'no'. One of her regulars came in and saw me. He asked my mother was I up for offer and she said no. They went on back, did their thing, and she stayed back there probably doing her drugs while he came back to the living room. Instead of walking out the door, he sat down next to me on the floor, offered me some drugs and tried to shove it down my throat when I said 'no'. I spat on his face, then he jumped on me." She stopped in front of her living room window and watched the cars drive by, but only saw the scared twelve year old from years ago. For years she played the same scene over and over in her mind, and for years the fear got worst.

"I screamed and screamed and screamed but my mother didn't hear me." By this time, I'neta was shaking and didn't even know it. Her mind was right back at that day and time. "This man had his hands up my shirt and was in the process of pulling down my pants when he went flying off of me. My father came home early because he was worried about me. Before I had a chance to stop my father, he had beaten the man with a crow bar. The man ended up in intensive care with severe brain damage. That's when my father got convicted of attempted murder. He claimed self-defense, but the judge didn't care about that. I try to see him every chance I get when I go home and he calls almost every other day. He has one more year before he can be released on parole and free to be here with me. For years I've said my mother should have been the one in prison, but..." She shrugged and found herself staring at her reflection on the window. "It's still hard sometimes to deal with, but my mother is trying. She gave up drugs, got saved, and got married to a very sweet man. And since I've gotten saved I can honestly say... I want to forgive her." She turned to see what his reaction was. *Maybe that he needs to grab his things and go.*

Well, I made it this far. I might as well say the rest. "So.. that's why I have a problem trusting people. I do blame my mother for what happened, and I do have a barrier up because of past relationships. The... the only person I know loves me with all of my issues is my father, and, of course, God. Everything you said that day was true and that's what scared me. I was afraid that maybe you used your advantage as a police officer to dig through my past, but..." She turned to look at her reflection again and dared herself to continue.

Opening up to a man was the hardest thing for her to do. What she really wanted was to run out of her own home and drive as far away as she can from these new feelings. She would sometimes allow herself to think maybe she and Joseph had a chance at something good; romantic dinners, laughs, kisses, everything but drama and pain. But she knew none of that fit into her life.

"But, what I'neta?" Joseph finally opened his mouth to say something. He didn't want to interrupt, afraid she would shut down and he would never know what went through that pretty head of hers.

She turned to look at him, squarely in the eye and exhaled. He saw every emotion she held in her eyes- fear, hope, doubt, and resolve. "But, we've been seeing each other for a while and I'm thinking..." *This is harder than I thought.* "I'm thinking maybe I need to start trusting you. But I need to know whether you can handle me with all of my issues."

Joseph sat on the couch staring at her for a long time. She didn't know how hard he was containing himself from grabbing her and holding her and declaring his undying love for her. He knew this was a huge step for her to take and was happy that she chose to take that step with him. He stood up slowly and made his way to where she was standing. She stood her ground and didn't budge, even when he got real close.

"I'neta, you are the most beautiful woman I've ever met, you're stronger than any person I know, and more trustworthy than anyone I've ever loved. And, yes, I do love you. I promise that I would never abuse you or make you feel inadequate. I promise to cherish you and respect you. I promise to be strong for you when you're at your worst. And I promise to give you my heart, if you will have it."

I'neta didn't know what to say. Stuff like this you read in romance books, not in real life. Especially not in her life. She waited for him to begin laughing and say 'sike' but it never came. All she saw was a look of adoration and sincerity, the same look her father gives her. She hugged him with all the strength she held in her and cried. She cried because for once in her life she felt loved, not just by God but also by a good man.

"I know it will take you some time to tell me you love me, but I know you do. I love you, I'neta, like I've never loved anyone before. I believe you are the jewel God has shaped to be mine for eternity, and I am so glad that He loves me enough to share you with me."

Joseph was right, I'neta was not going to declare her unwavering love for him at that moment, but in due time, there would be no doubt about who she would want to spend the rest of her life with.

* * *

Joyce was awaiting Mr. Mariano at Monty's restaurant. She sat reading over the documents to make sure she had everything on track. Mr. Mariano walked in fifteen minutes late, with a bouquet of flowers in his hand, and his breath reeking of alcohol. "I am so sorry I'm late, Joyce. I was held up at another business meeting." He plopped himself down across from her, and handed her the bouquet of red roses. "Here, these are for you."

"Thank you, Mr. Mariano, but that is not necessary." Laying the flowers on the table, she brushed it to the side. "And please call me Ms. Nickerson."

"Why so formal? We are on a date, no?"

"This is business, Mr. Mariano. Strictly business," Joyce said, feeling just a little uncomfortable.

"A business dinner. A date. Same thing," Mr. Mariano said, waving his hand to signal the waiter. "Do you drink champagne?"

"No, thank you. I prefer to keep a clear mind while doing business," Joyce said, shuffling the documents around to give him the hint. "Plus, seems like you have had enough to drink already."

"Oh, you can never get enough of celebrating. Relax... have some fun. Enjoy life. You're about to sign a new contract that may change the way this city looks at your business. I can guarantee many more clientele for you. Now, again, what kind of champagne would you like?"

Both Mr. Mariano and the waiter were waiting on her response. She remembered drinking while in college, and that was something she desperately did not want to go back to. *Father, please help me right now. I don't want to go back to how I was. Would you make a way of escape for me... please?*

"Actually, Sir," the waiter interjected, "we've run out of champagne. There was a bad accident in the pantry earlier today and everything stored there was destroyed, including the champagnes.

We are expecting another shipment tomorrow. Until then, all we have to offer is sweet tea, coffee, water, and fountain drinks. My apologies."

"Well, looks like we may have to celebrate another time. In the mean while, I will take a cup of dark coffee with a teaspoon of sugar."

"And I will have the same, with lots of cream, please," Joyce responded, very thankful that God heard her. *Thank you, Lord.*

The waiter walked away and before Mr. Mariano could suggest anything else that did not pertain to business, Joyce quickly opened the documents in her hand and flipped through them. "Now, I would like you to read through these documents and sign every highlighted area. It is the same copy I faxed you earlier this week, but if you would like to go through any specifics I would be glad to walk through them with you." Joyce went straight to business.

"Wow! You mean what you say, don't you? Business, business, business. Why don't we take a breather? Tell me something about yourself." Mr. Mariano pushed the papers aside so she couldn't reach them except by touching his hand.

"You want to know something about me?" The words were laced with cynicism, but Mariano ignored it nevertheless.

"Yes. You are a very beautiful and charming woman. What else goes on in that," he focused his gaze on her bosom, then back to her eyes, "head of yours?"

"Well, let's see. I love to dance, I love to sing, and I love to skate. Best of all," she leaned closer and said in a whisper, "I also don't have time for foolish games. So, how about we get back to business here." She leaned back against her chair and crossed her arms.

"Mmm, testy. I like a woman with fire in her eyes and attitude. Usually, what I like is what I want. And eventually, what I want is what I get."

"Mr. Mariano, let's get one thing straight. I will never get involve with a client... before, during, or after a contract. So, if what you personally want is me, then maybe what you corporately need is another contractor."

"You will not sign on this contract all because I find you to be an irresistible woman?"

"No. I will not sign on this contract because you cannot seem to control your appetite for a beautiful woman, even for the sake of your business. I have never tolerated a come-on from a client and still have very low tolerance for those who cannot catch a clue." Joyce reached across to take the contract and placed it in her briefcase. "Maybe we need to give you a night to compose yourself and discuss this in the morning. You seemed to have had a little too much to drink before arriving here. Have your secretary call mine and we'll set another date. Good evening."

She walked out leaving Mr. Mariano sitting alone at the table with two cups of coffee, a bouquet of roses, and smiling at her exit. She had never felt this disturbed or annoyed by a client before. There was a lot riding on this project, but she would rather start from scratch, than allow anyone to harass her. Usually clients catch on and cease pursuing, but this one was very persistent.

She reached for her keys to unlock her car door when a pair of arms reached around her, entrapping her against her door. She had enough room to turn, and she did to come face to face with Mr. Mariano's daunting smile.

"I do not take no for an answer very easily, Ms. Nickerson. I was very serious when I say I usually get what I want. And just in case I didn't make myself clear… I want you."

"Just in case I didn't make myself clear, Mr. Mariano, I do not want you, nor am I available to be taken. I advise you to take your arms from around me so I can get into my vehicle."

"And if I choose not to?"

"You would regret ever leaving Italy to come to the United States."

Without hesitation, she quickly tried to knee him in the crotch, but he quickly averted himself so that she grazed his thigh with her knee.

He chuckled at her defense tactic and grabbed her arm, "You American women are so predictable. Now, let me show you how persistent an Italian man could be." For someone intoxicated, he was very strong and seemed physically stable to do anything.

Before she knew it, he was dragging her away from her car kicking and screaming, while the other patrons inside the restaurant were clueless about what was happening less than eighteen feet away.

✳ ✳ ✳

"All right, Baby. I have to get going. I need to head to the station to pick up some paperwork before heading home." Joseph and I'neta finished the movie, not even sure what the picture was about. He looked at his watch and realized it was going on nine, and he still had some police reports to complete before work the next day. He stood up and lifted I'neta up with him, giving her a gentle hug and a kiss on the forehead. He resisted the urge to kiss her lips that always seemed to be calling his name. *If she only knew how hard it was to control that urge.* "Do I get to see you tomorrow?"

Lord, this man does some weird, nice things to my body. Help me to be strong. "You most definitely will. Didn't you promise me a picnic?"

"A picnic it is, but it'll have to be indoors since I won't be getting off of work until six."

"OK. And maybe we can go bike riding on Saturday or take a walk on the beach. Something."

"Yeah, we'll do something. Well, I have to get going," he said, reaching over to give her another hug. "Love you." The way she looked up at him with that twinkle in her eyes made him want to kiss her. *A soft peck wouldn't hurt anything.*

She saw how he longingly looked at her lips, and decided to meet him half way for their first kiss as a couple. He first brushed her lips softly with his, not sure how deep he should take it. She sighed against his lips, and wrapped her arms around his neck. The closer she got, the tighter he wrapped his arms around her, and the deeper the kiss got.

Be careful.

He saw the words flash across his mind, and quickly pulled away. Taking two steps back, it took him a few seconds to compose himself. "I'm sorry."

"For what? That felt nice." I'neta said.

"It did, but ... I don't want to put us in a compromising situation."

"Oh, don't think too hard about it, Joseph. It was just a kiss." She closed the gap between them and wrapped her arm around his waist. "A goodnight's kiss that was long overdue."

He smiled at her and gave her one last kiss on her forehead before peeling her arms from around him. "Woman, you underestimate the power you have. And with that said, I have to go."

She walked him out and watched him drive off with a smile plastered on her face. A clear sign that she was growing to care for this man. She probably won't be declaring her love for him tomorrow, but it will come soon enough.

She wiped down her kitchen counters and fluffed her pillows, all with thoughts of tomorrow's picnic. *I wonder if he'll kiss me like that again. He has such soft lips and the way he holds me...* Her thoughts were interrupted by the sound of her phone ringing. She sucked her teeth at the interruption and answered the annoying gadget.

"Hello?"

"Hey, I'neta. It's Clint. I hope I didn't wake you."

"No, not at all. What's up?"

"Is Joyce with you by any chance?" Clint asked, sounding a little worried.

"No. Why?"

"Well, she was supposed to call me after her business meeting tonight, which should have ended about two hours ago, but she has not. She's not answering her phone, so I was hoping maybe she stopped at your place for a few."

"No, she didn't. Since when have you been this worried about her?"

"It's not like that. Ms. Ruby called me earlier about the guy she was meeting with. Said she had a weird feeling about him, and wanted to join them for dinner at Monty's, but Joyce refused. She said she was going to have a drink, be there for probably thirty minutes then head home. Usually, I don't worry, but something doesn't feel right."

"All right. Let's not get ahead of ourselves, Clint," I'neta attempted to calm him down in order to not start panicking herself. "Her meeting probably lasted longer than she expected. I'll call the restaurant and see if she's still there. All right?"

"All right. Call me back."

She hung up and called Monty's. It took them a while to answer, but when they did she did not receive an answer favorable to her question.

"Hey Paul. This is I'neta. How are you?"

"Well, hello sweet thang. I am good. I haven't seen you in a few weeks," the host responded cheerfully.

"Been too busy. Look... have you seen Joyce tonight?"

"Yes, ma'am. I believe she left about an hour or two ago. She left kind of angry, but her gentleman friend must have apologized when he followed her out because they left together in his car. Her vehicle is still here, and she will have to pick it up before the evening is out."

"Thank you. I'll make sure she does that. Could you tell me what kind of car he was driving?"

"I believe it was a black Mustang. She didn't seem too happy getting into the car with him, especially through the driver's side. As a matter of fact, seemed like he shoved her in, but I try to keep away from domestic situations. What goes on in their house stays in their house."

"If a woman doesn't seem comfortable leaving with a man, why not call the police?" Now I'neta was becoming worried. "Oh, never mind. This is a waste of time. Thank you."

She quickly hung up the phone and called Joseph.

"Miss me already," he said, answering the phone. "It's only been, what... a little over ten minutes."

"Get over yourself. Joyce is missing," she said frantically. She didn't know what to do with herself. Hundreds of thoughts ran across her mind, but she refused to entertain any of them. *Lord, please let her be okay. Please.*

"What do you mean?"

"She's missing, Joseph. She left the restaurant about two hours ago, but the maître d' said she left with her guest and seemed like she didn't want to. She left pretty upset and he followed her out. What if he did something to her, Joseph?"

"All right. Calm down. You never know. Maybe they cleared things up and decided to have dinner elsewhere."

"Joseph, Joyce does not get into anyone's car that she does not know. Especially if they have to shove her in through the driver's side. Something's not right, at all."

"I'll check it out, okay, I'neta. But don't worry. Pray." He hung up with her and that's exactly what she did... pray. She called Clint and let him know what was going on. What he did after that, she doesn't know. She didn't want to waste anymore time speaking to someone else other than God.

chapter 17

JOSEPH FLEW TO the station like someone was on his tail. He was driving a rental instead of the squad car, so he wasn't able listen in to any calls from the dispatcher. He made it to the police station in one piece, knowing that he broke a few laws on the way there. *Forgive me, Father.* Once he walked into the station, he looked around to see if he would see Joyce among the small crowd, then went to the dispatcher to see if anyone called in a rape, kidnapping, or assault. When the answer came up negative, he was relieved yet worried because there hadn't been any sign of Joyce. He sat down at one of his colleague's desk, not knowing what to do. *God, please help me. Let Joyce be okay, and if she's not show me how to find her.* He laid his head down, praying for the peace of mind of everyone, and hoping the situation was not as bad as it seemed.

"Joseph," a weary and trembling voice interrupted his prayer. He looked up to see Joyce standing in front of him, clothes ripped, hair everywhere, blood on her shirt, and too many scratches and bruises on her arms and face. He stood up and gently placed her into a seat.

"Are you okay?" *Thank you, Father, for letting her be alive.*

"Name is Victor... Mariano. We were supposed to have dinner... to discuss business... came drunk. He snatched me... forced me in his car... small gun. I jumped... out. I think... he shot me... heard gunshots... I don't know," she sounded like she was getting weaker. "I came here... because... it... was closer... and... you..."

Joseph's heart went still as she fell off the seat and unto the floor.

✳ ✳ ✳

"Is she okay?" I'neta and Clint both rushed into the hospital searching for Joseph, and found him sitting with his head down. I'neta sat next to him, but Clint paced up and down the corridor.

All three fought the thought that Joyce may not make it. They knew God was able to change situations, but He also had His will and who's to say His will was for Joyce to live. They could only hope.

Joseph gave I'neta a worried look, then responded. "The doctor said the scrapes and bruises were from her jumping out of the speeding car. She did fracture a few ribs and twisted her ankle in the process. The worst part is," he looked up at them, "she got shot in the stomach. The idiot shot at her when she jumped out of his car. They have her in surgery right now and say it may be a few hours before they can let us know anything. The last I heard, the nurse told me they are working on extracting the bullet, but it's causing more bleeding and she has already lost a lot of blood. They're afraid she may be hemorrhaging."

"Oh, my God." I'neta grabbed her stomach in panic. *God, I do not want to charge you falsely, but how could you let this happen? Why didn't you protect her?*

Clint froze mid step, struggling with the fearful thoughts bombarding his mind. He so desperately needed to trust God right now, but the situation was not looking good. *Lord, I'm finding it hard right now to believe she'll be okay when all the evidence is proving otherwise.*

All things work together for good to those who love God.

Clint heard the scripture play over in his mind, but he was too worried to listen. *Please work this out, God. She just came back to you. I'm sure there's more she can do for you. She's already been through a lot. Give her a chance to love and serve you the way that we all know she can. Let her live, please.*

Clint moved to stand in front of one of the side windows, and touched his forehead to the glass. "Are you guys looking for the guy?" he asked.

"Of course we are. There's an APB out on him, but we don't have much to go by except his name and his car," Joseph said.

"Are the doctors able to tell us what was hit by the bullet? Were there any major damages in any organs?" I'neta started to think of all the issues Joyce could have. Crazy thoughts like, would she be able to have children or eat anything ever again, rolled through her mind. She didn't want to worry, but it seemed like the easiest thing to do in this situation.

"They won't be able to tell us anything until after surgery." He reached over to grasp her hand, wishing he can take away the tension he saw on her face. "I'm sure everything will be just fine, I'neta," Joseph said.

"Well, no need sitting around here worrying," Clint said. "Let's pray."

Clint pulled a chair directly in front of Joseph and I'neta. There were lots of emotions flowing around- fear, doubt, hope. They held hands and bowed their heads, lifting their dear friend, Joyce, in prayer.

❄ ❄ ❄

"The doctor said they were able to remove the bullet. Nothing was punctured nor were there any damages to major organs. The problem is they cannot stop the bleeding, and they're not sure what's causing her to bleed so much. It could be a few more hours before they get back to us with anything." I'neta came back into the waiting room, providing Clint and Joseph the bitter sweet news.

It had been three hours since they'd been sitting there waiting on a report from the doctor. Joseph had not yet completed the reports he had to do, Clint missed his movie, and I'neta only had a few hours of sleep, but neither one of them

would choose to be anywhere else. The cops were still out looking for Mariano, but they knew he'd be caught in due time.

"I praise God Joyce was smart enough to jump out when
she could. Who knows what this guy was going to do to her
after… " Clint couldn't finish his sentence. "What I would like
is a few minutes alone with him. Just me and him." The anger he
felt inside was something new for him. Over the last few months
his feelings for Joyce developed into something more, and he felt
like he was almost cheated in figuring out where this was going.
*I don't know when, but I started to love this woman as a woman, Lord.
Don't take that away from me.*

He covered his face with his hands, feeling helpless. "Just
when I thought… I can't lose her."

Both I'neta and Joseph looked at Clint in disbelief, never
hearing him sound so down and depressed. Clint was always the
strong one, the one who would always find the right words at
the right time to help the right person. But looking at him now,
with his body slouched over and his face buried in his hands,
anyone would think he was having a mid-life crisis.

I'neta went and knelt before him, taking him into her
arms, and allowing him to hold her in return. He wrapped his
arms around her, buried his head on her shoulder and wept. For a
brief moment Clint let go of pride, responsibility, and strength.
He didn't worry about how men shouldn't cry in public, about
being strong for everyone, or showing how to have faith and
hope. For once, he let it go and let someone else deal with it.

They weren't sure how long they stayed in that position,
but when the doctor entered the waiting room, I'neta's legs were
cramped from kneeling, and Clint had stopped crying.

Not sure how to share this information with a small
group of concerned friends, Dr. Wilkens cleared his throat before
saying, "I'm afraid I have a bit of bad news. We're having a hard
time keeping the hemorrhaging under control. She's in the same
predicament she was in before, minus the bullet. She's losing too
much blood and that may cause severe…" He wasn't able to keep
his voice from breaking, seeing the look of devastation in their
eyes. He watched as they prayed for hours, and found it hard to

break their hearts. "Nothing is definite about her state. What I do suggest is that you continue to pray as you have been doing. I'll send word as soon as I get something definite." He walked away trying to hold on to the tears forming in his eyes, worried that maybe this time prayer may not work for his patient.

chapter 18

IT WAS SUNDAY morning, three days since Joyce had been in the hospital. She was still in the Intensive Care Unit, unresponsive but not comatose. After sitting in the waiting room for twenty-two hours, Dr. Wilkens finally convinced all three friends to go home and get some rest. I'neta had been to see Joyce every day hoping to receive better news, but the situation never changed.

I'neta was at home preparing to attend church with Joseph. This would be the first time she'd attended church in almost ten years. She tried on five different blouses with her black peasant skirt, still not sure which one to wear. She stood inside her walk-in closet staring at her wall, contemplating whether she really wanted to do this. *You have to. There's no other way you can stay saved without spiritual guidance.*

Everyone needs a shepherd, she could hear her mother saying. *Yes, the Lord is our shepherd, but He also sends leaders, pastors, shepherds in this world to help guide us and lead us in this holy walk with Him, Net. Find the right one and get connected to him.*

She exhaled the breath she was holding and finally chose a yellow and white sundress. By the time she got ready, Joseph was knocking on her door. She took one more look in the mirror and evaluated her makeup, the turquoise pearl necklace, bracelet, and tear drop earrings she used to accessorize her dress, her turquoise pumps, and her pinned-up hair to make sure she wasn't giving signs that suggested anything inappropriate. She grabbed her purse, her keys, and the study Bible Joyce recently bought her, stopped at the door to exhale one more time before pasting a smile on her face and swinging it wide open.

Joseph stood there with all six feet, two inches and two hundred pounds covered in a grey suit, white collar shirt, and salmon color tie and hanky. *How can a man look that sexy going to church*, I'neta asked herself as she assessed him from top to bottom. He gave her a smile that lit up her heart and gave a slight bow.

"Good morning, My Gorgeous Lady. Are you ready to attend service with me?" He tried to use a fake English accent, but it came out sounding more like Count Dracula. Acting was never one of his strong qualities, but it never stopped him from trying.

"Good morning to you." She closed the door behind her and locked it shut before she changed her mind. She was too nervous to laugh at his lameness, so she gave him a bright smile and a kiss on the cheek. "I'm willing and ready. By the way, you look rather..." She wasn't sure how to describe how handsome he was.

"Ravishing. Enticing. Fine." Joseph decided to help her.

"Uh... no. Not exactly what I was looking for. More like... handsome. What time are we supposed to be there, by the way?" She allowed him to take her hands and escort her to his Chrysler. He helped her into the car and got in himself before answering her question.

"Well, service starts at eleven but I wanted to have breakfast with you first. Which is why I asked you to be ready by eight thirty. And ready you are. Ain't that somethin'!" Joseph always teased I'neta about how much time it takes her to get ready. Little did he know she had to be up at 6:30 this morning just to be ready on time.

"Whoever worked on your car did an awesome job," I'neta commented.

"Looks just like new. You wouldn't think just a few months ago someone pounded the mess out of it. And it was cheap to repair."

"Good for you."

Joseph took her to a small, yet decent, restaurant that served breakfast only. They had the best omelet I'neta had ever tasted and their fruit were fresh and sweet. Joseph tried having small talk while they were eating, but she was too nervous to concentrate on anything he was asking her.

"Why are you so nervous?" Joseph finally asked once they were done.

"Because... it has been a while since I've been to church, and..." she took a slow, deep breath. Her nerves were really getting out of control and she had to get it together. *Come on, I'neta. We're over that stage. You survived it all and now you have another chance at life. Forget the past, for behold, God is doing a new thing. Just help me, Father. Where I am weak, you are stronger.* "I'll be fine. Just jitters."

"Just jitters, huh," he pushed his seat back and stood up. "Well, Ms. Jitters, it's time for us to get going. Shall we be on our way?" He watched fear and doubt pool in her eyes, then saw it replaced with confidence. She smiled at him and gave him her hand to help her up. After paying for their meal, he led her to his car and to the last place she thought she would come back to.

❋ ❋ ❋

I'neta fell in love with the praise and worship team the moment she stepped into the church. It was like being at a live concert, but anointed. From the singers to the musicians, the dancers, the audience, and the children dancing in the aisles, no one could say God wasn't in that place. A dark skinned man, medium built and slightly balding, sat on the pulpit with his eyes shut, and bobbed his head and his feet to the music, while a woman stood to his left with hands raised. Everyone seemed to be in pure... worship.

A sweet middle age woman ushered Joseph and I'neta to the third row, next to two young women with their arms up in worship. The one closest greeted I'neta with a hug. At any other time, sitting this far up would have been uncomfortable, but at this moment she felt at home. She placed her purse on the seat next to her, stayed standing, and joined the others in worship.

She closed her eyes and lifted her hands as far up as she could. *Lord, I thank you so much for life. Thank you for saving me. Thank you for not giving up on me. Thank you for another chance with you. Thank you! Thank you! Thank you! I love you so much. You are great and greatly to be praise. Your greatness is unsearchable. I praise you and adore you. I love you and honor you. You are my king, my joy, my love, my salvation, my life. There is none like you. Hallelujah, Father. Hallelujah!*

Joseph looked at I'neta and saw how easy it was for her to join the worship. The love he felt for her grew more at that moment. *I love to see a woman who is unashamed to praise God. Thank you, Father.* He smiled, shut his eyes, and joined everyone else in worship. With his baritone voice and her alto pitch, they both sounded lovely together in unison, praising God.

I'neta doesn't know how long they stayed in this position. The singers were now singing a soft melody, the musicians played like they heard from heaven, some of the dancers were bent over in worship, while some danced, and the rest cried. Even the children in the aisles had their hands up in worship, screaming 'Hallelujah'. Those seated in the audience were either bent over, arms up in surrender, on their knees, or swaying back and forth to the music, eyes closed and lips moving. The man sitting in the pulpit stood up and took the microphone from the lead singer. He signaled them to leave the pulpit and waited for them to do so before opening his mouth to speak.

Joseph leaned over and whispered in her ear, "That's Pastor Willis. And the woman sitting next to him is his wife, Joanne Willis."

I'neta nodded as if she guessed it all along and looked up at the pastor as he started to speak to the congregation.

"What we need to understand is God looks for those who will worship Him in spirit and in truth. He doesn't just want accolades flowing out of your mouth, or hands up without surrender. He wants pure, unadulterated worship. Not from your arms, not from your lips, but from your heart. Everyone, lift your hands, open your heart and your mouth to give Him praise. Forget about yourself... forget about your troubles... forget about whatever may be waiting at home for you. Just lift your hearts in worship and see how God takes care of the rest." Pastor Willis shut his eyes and lifted his hands in surrender.

The musicians continued to play a soft melody while everyone else raised their voices in worship. I'neta never had this experience, so she was unsure what to do with herself. She bent over but that didn't seem to do the trick, she raised her hands but felt like she should do more. She finally gave in to kneeling down at her seat. She wasn't distracted with anyone's voice, nor did she have to worry about others staring at her. It was just her and God.

"God you are so awesome. I bless you and I thank you. You are God and God alone. There is no one before you. I give you glory and honor. My king, my life. My Alpha and my Omega... my beginning and my end." The same feeling I'neta felt that night she got saved in her home overtook her. This time it wasn't Joseph's arms embracing her... it was God's. That day she drew closer to God, and there was no turning back as far as she was concerned.

❋ ❋ ❋

On that same Sunday morning, Clint went to service and listened to his pastor preach about faith and trust in God's will. He tried to hold on to hope and trust, and each time he felt the weight and fear of Joyce's life hanging on the balance lift from his shoulders, the last conversation he had with the doctor yesterday played in his mind.

How is she holding up, Doctor, Clint remembered asking.

Honestly, Son... she's still not responding to us. Good news is we were able to finally stop the bleeding. Do you go to church?

Surprised at the doctor's question, Clint nodded his head.

Then I suggest you go home, get a good night's rest, and go to church tomorrow morning. The nurse station has your number and if anything changes we will get in touch with you. Dr. Wilkens grasped Clint's shoulder and looked him in the eye. *This is a good time to trust in the God you believe in. Our faith is what moves God, Son.*

With that said, Dr. Wilkens squeezed Clint's shoulder one last time and walked away. Clint went to see Joyce before leaving the hospital. Seeing her helpless and lying still was not something he could get use to. He moved to her side and brushed a soft kiss on her forehead.

Before walking away, he whispered in her ear, "You can't leave me now, Joyce. Not when I've finally realized what I have with you here. Come back to me, Love." He kissed her forehead again and left.

Sitting in service now, he prayed his faith would move God in saving Joyce's life. *Father... I'm just now realizing who she is to me. I don't believe you'll reveal that, then take her away. I'm trusting in you to be God and pray that my faith moves you to work on Joyce's behalf.*

During alter call, he went to kneel before God, praying that his action showed his faith and Joyce would stay in his life.

chapter 19

I'NETA, CLINT, AND Joseph sat in the hospital's waiting room waiting for the doctor to complete testing on Joyce. They haven't found why she had not been responsive and were planning to call in a specialist to take more tests. They checked for brain activity, heart rate, and blood pressure like they've done within the last few days, and still were not able to come up with an answer. All three sat patiently within their own thoughts, waiting to be told they could go in to see Joyce.

I'neta looked at both men and asked the question that's been swimming around in her mind. "Do you think she'll make it out alive? I can't help but think she finally gave her life to God because her time to leave was coming."

Clint looked at I'neta and forced a smile on his face. "She's still here. That's what matters. She's still here so that means she still has a chance. God don't save people just because their life is going to end, I'neta. We have to believe all this is going to work out for her good. Her good and ours."

I'neta soaked in what Clint said in order to keep believing this will work out for their good. They sat silently for nearly half an hour before the nurse came for them. One by one, they slowly stood up and walked down the hallway to Joyce's room.

The EKG monitor beeped softly on the side of her bed, white sheet covered her from chest to feet, and an IV stuck in her arm. Looking at her, one would think she was softly asleep. I'neta went to stand beside her and softly brushed Joyce's left hand.

"Joyce, your vacation has lasted long enough. It's time for you to come back. Ok." I'neta controlled the tears that threatened to roll down her face.

Joseph stood behind I'neta while Clint went to stand on the other side of Joyce. Clint brushed the side of Joyce's face before saying, "Why is it your vacation is making us tired? I swear you owe me one when you get back here. Seriously, Joyce, I agree with I'neta. It's time for you to come back."

Joseph moved to stand next to I'neta and grabbed her hand. "How about we say a short prayer."

I'neta reached across Joyce to grab Clint's hand, then bowed her head. Joseph's voice rose above the beep of the monitor. "Father, we thank you for the opportunity to come to you in prayer on behalf of our friend. We stand on your word that you can do all things, and you are able to do exceeding abundantly above all that we ask or think. We ask that you will heal Joyce and you will bring her back to us. We pray that every organ, every vessel, every body part will work according to how you've purposed for it to work. We believe you are a God that hears and answers our prayers. We thank you in advance for the miracle you will perform through Joyce. It's in Jesus' name we pray and agree, Amen!"

Joseph ended the prayer and all three stood still as the monitor sound went from beeping to a solid loud screech. Before they had a chance to respond, nurses were pushing them out the room and yelling codes to each other.

I'neta reached for Joseph in the hall and sobbed on his shoulders, while Clint slid on the floor leaning against the wall as the monitor showed Joyce flat lined.

✳ ✳ ✳

While the doctor and nurses helped Joyce fight for her life, Clint, I'neta, and Joseph sat in the waiting room praying. They sat in silence, not having the energy to speak words of encouragement to each other, and not giving up faith to ask the question they all were thinking.

A few times they got up to ask the nurses for an update, and each time nothing could be shared. The only hope they held on to was that no one had come out to announce Joyce's death.

Two hours later, a doctor came into the waiting room and walked towards the three friends, with their heads bent in prayer. He cleared his throat and all three quickly jumped up.

"Is she... is she okay, Dr. Snider?" I'neta asked with anxiety showing on her face.

Dr. Snider was the doctor on duty that day and just met the three friends a few hours ago. The faith and care they showed towards their friend amazed him. He cleared his throat and answered, "We were able to get her heart beating again on its own. She gave us a scare a few times, but looks like she's pulling through."

I'neta sank to her seat and released a long breath. Tears flowed down her face as she murmured *Thank you, God*, over and over again. Joseph stood next to her and rubbed her shoulders as the doctor continued.

"Great news is she woke up for a brief moment, said she was thirsty then fell asleep. We did a few tests and she's responding to stimuli. She seems very tired so I am going to ask that you all save your visits for tomorrow and give her time to rest."

Joseph and Clint nodded in agreement while I'neta continued to cry tears of joy. Joseph crouched in front of her and circled his arms around her. Clint sat on his seat amazed how at the most extreme moment God stepped in.

God, I thank you so much for being a God who always answers prayers.

❋ ❋ ❋

Joyce lolled on the hospital bed in more pain than she had ever been in. *If this is how it feels to have a baby, Lord, I pass.* She tried to position herself in a more comfortable way, but every move seemed to make the pain worst. *Maybe I just need to be still, cause this is not working.* She reached to the side of the bed to buzz the nurse, who came running in with a bright smile.

"Ms. Nickerson, good to see you're awake," Nurse Kathy reached over to check her stats and heart rate, which showed to be normal. "I'll go get Dr. Wilkens." The nurse started to run out the room until Joyce called her back.

"Can I get something to drink, please? I'm a little thirsty." A little wasn't even the word. Seemed like every part of her body felt dry. Her throat, her eyes, her bones, and from the looks of her ashy feet, so were they.

The nurse came back with a jug of ice water with cups and straws, followed by Dr. Wilkens.

"Well, good morning. Good to see you in the land of the living." He greeted her with a smile before poking her body in places, making her squirm in pain. The nurse tried to have her sip the water she asked for, but the pain was too terrible for her to focus on anything else. While the doctor gave her apologetic smiles, Joyce kept twitching her face away from the straw being probed into her face.

"Would you please stop!" Joyce yelled. She didn't mean to scream, but she was getting frustrated.

"Nurse Kathy, would you just step to the side for just a moment. I'm sure when Ms. Nickerson gets ready to drink something, she'll ask for it. Okay?" His tone wasn't condescending or harsh, but it made the nurse flinch as if slapped. He turned to check Joyce's heart beat and was amazed at how strong it was. "Seems like we have a miracle on our hands. Your vital signs are back to normal and your heart beat is strong. You may feel a little weak still, but you'll be just fine. We will have to run some more tests to make sure you're not having any internal bleeding, but from the looks of things, I would say God has answered your friends' prayers. Other than some soreness and a dry throat, how do you feel?"

"Like I was ran over by an eighteen wheeler... twice. Can I get a drink of water now?"

The nurse cautiously approached her with the cup at hand. She allowed Joyce to take a sip from the cup before placing it on the desk next to her. Joyce saw how nervous the nurse was and felt somewhat bad about her outburst.

Not understanding why, Joyce had an overwhelming need to apologize when she looked at the nurse and realized she was trying her best to not cry. Once the doctor was done checking Joyce's blood pressure, he walked away with the nurse in tow. Before the nurse could walk completely out the room, Joyce called her back.

"Yes? What else do you need, Ms. Nickerson?" Nurse Kathy had a little edge to her voice, which made Joyce feel worse.

"I just wanted to say I'm sorry. I shouldn't have yelled." Joyce watched the nurse look at her with a blank stare.

Suddenly, she exhaled a long breath and gave Joyce a sad smile. "Today has not been one of my best days. I had three other patients to complain about me to Dr. Wilkens. All because I wouldn't allow them to leave the premises for a smoke. Of course that's not what they told him, so... I've been trying to stay on my p's and q's with him. Lately..." She shook her head and sighed again. "Thank you for apologizing. It really means a lot."

"I only did what was right." Joyce's eye lids seemed to be drooping on their own, and Nurse Kathy seemed to be drifting farther away. "I am really sorry," was the last thing she said before giving in to the heaviness of her eyes and the sweetness of sleep.

※ ※ ※

"So, has Mariano been caught yet?" Clint asked.

Clint, Joseph, and I'neta were sitting in the waiting room as Joyce went through her regular routine with the doctor's probing. Joseph was providing I'neta with an update on Mason's search, which was showing unsuccessful. As concerned as Joseph was about I'neta's safety, Clint was about Joyce's... if not more. He turned to face Joseph and waited for an answer.

"Yes. Well... actually, he turned himself in. He explained everything was a mistake that night. He just wanted to scare Joyce. But when she jumped out the car, his instinct was to grab her, and that's how the gun went off. He wasn't sure whether he'd hit her, but he was too afraid to stop and check. We charged him with possession of a firearm and kidnapping. He's spending at least ten years in prison for just the firearm charge alone."

Joseph was proud of the arrest, but was more bothered that Mason hadn't been found yet.

While Clint and Joseph discussed other charges Joyce could file against Mariano, I'neta sat thinking about the entire situation. She didn't want to question God's decision about allowing Mariano to be caught and not Mason, but for her it didn't quite make sense. She believed Mason to be more of a threat than Mariano, yet he's the one still on the run.

Not enjoying where these thoughts were taking her, she shook off the dreary feeling, and tried to focus on how happy she was that Joyce was still alive.

Seeing the intense look on I'neta's face, Joseph placed an arm around her shoulders, "A penny for your thoughts?"

She gave him a weak smile, "I'm fine, Sweetheart. What about you? Were you able to get some work done?"

"Yes. But of course I had more placed on my desk this morning. Are you ready to head in and see Joyce?"

"Oh... yeah. I didn't know the doctor came out?"

"I know. You were deep in thought. Anything you want to share?"

"Not right now. Let's go see Joyce." She preceded the men to the room and knocked before entering. "I hope you're decent because I'm not alone." She announced while walking into the room. The men stayed behind and waited for Joyce to welcome them in.

"I am fully clothed and wrapped tight under these sheets. I feel like I'm in a straight jacket. How are you guys doing?"

Joseph walked in, receiving a smile from Joyce. Clint followed, first taking a look around the room before his eyes landed on Joyce. There were flowers everywhere. A huge balloon clung to a fruit basket not too far from Joyce's head. Joyce lied propped up, looking beautiful as ever. Their eye contact spoke volumes before Clint cleared his throat and commanded it to work.

"Hey," was all he could say. He took the chair closest to her bed and gently caressed her hand. "How are you?"

Joyce forgot there were two other people in the room as she got pulled in by the intensity of Clint's eyes. Everything he didn't say with his mouth showed in his eyes. "I'm well. Thanks for the flowers. They're beautiful." She wanted to pull her hand away from his grasp because it was doing strange things to her. It was hard enough her throat went dry when he stepped into the room, now she couldn't seem to focus on what he was saying.

I'neta grasped Joyce's other hand and massaged it. "Are you okay? Do you need anything?"

"OK. Let's get this straight right now," Joyce looked at all three of her friends and knew they really cared for her. "Please don't come in here with this soppy mess. I'm still alive and not dead. Yes, I'm in pain, but hey... let's thank God that I can feel pain. I do not want to see one teary eye, not one more sympathetic gaze, not one more," taking her hand away from I'neta, "hand massage. OK?" Looking at all three. "OK?"

"OK," they all said in unison.

"Seems like you're back to your normal self. That bullet didn't change anything." Clint said sarcastically before leaning in to kiss her cheek. He lingered a little longer before pulling away.

"It surely didn't," Joyce said in a whisper, a little confused about the contact.

She looked into Clint's eyes and knew what she saw there was different than what she was use to seeing. The way his thumb kept brushing across her knuckles and how close he allowed their face to be spoke volumes. She could only hope by the look in his eyes, he was serious about what his actions were saying. She wished she was alone with him to ask all the questions that were running through her mind. To ask him whether his feelings for her has changed, or whether it was the fear of losing her that caused him to act this way? Was he attracted to her because he now realized what he has, or was she just the closest thing to a girlfriend since his break up? She wanted to know the answers to these questions, but knew she couldn't handle the rejection in front of others if he denied any affection for her.

I'neta cleared her throat and broke Clint and Joyce's eye contact. "How long do you have before you can leave here?" I'neta asked concerned.

"About two weeks. I have to go through physical therapy and all that good stuff to make sure I'm fit to go." The look on her face turned from peaceful to fearful within seconds. "Have... have Mariano been found?"

Joseph was the one to answer her question. "Yes, he has, and trust... he'll be in prison for a very long time. You don't have to worry about anything."

"Thank you, Joseph. I don't know—"

She was interrupted by the television speakers blasting with gospel music. I'neta held both the television and the bed remote control in her hands. "Alright, enough of this soppy mess. It's karaoke time, and yes, that means everyone has to participate." She lifted the bed remote control up in the air for Joyce to see. "Especially you or you'll be tortured with having to do sit ups while lying in bed. And I'm sure that can be very painful for someone who just had stomach surgery."

"You wouldn't dare?" Joyce looked at her friend in pure shock.

"Try me if you wanna." I'neta pointed the remote towards her and lifted up an eyebrow. She really didn't have the guts to hurt her friend, and Joyce knew it, but she went along with the game once Clint and Joseph started holding a competition on who could be the loudest singer.

Joyce tried to hold back her laughter as she watched her three friends. *Only friends like mine would be sitting in a hospital interrupting the peace with their loud singing.* She felt so much love for them and knew if it wasn't for God's grace and their prayers she wouldn't have made it out alive. She smiled and joined in with the singing once I'neta pointed the remote at her as a threat, casting the gentlest smile on her face.

chapter 20

"ARE YOU SURE you don't want me to carry you into the house?" Clint had been bickering over Joyce ever since he picked her up from the hospital. She would have called I'neta but she knew she needed Clint's man power, plus, in all honesty, she wanted to see him again. They really needed to discuss what was happening between them. She just didn't know he would be this annoying.

"Clint, I know you're trying to help, but please let me try this on my own. I promise if I show any sign of pain or stumbling, you can pick me up. OK?"

Clint hesitated, then decided it would be best to do as she asked for now, instead of doing it Mandingo style. So, reluctantly, he stood behind her with his hands on her elbow. They made it up her three small steps and into her house without her collapsing. She dropped herself on the couch and threw the crutches on the floor.

"The doctor didn't lie when he said we use our stomach muscles for almost everything. Even sitting down was a little strenuous." She looked at Clint leaning against her front door, watching her with so much adoration in his eyes.

"You are such a beautiful woman, you know that," he slowly started his way towards her.

"Well, thank you, but this beautiful woman is feeling a little parched right now. Would you mind grabbing me a bottle of water from the fridge? Please."

She watched him change his course and turned towards her kitchen. Everything about him screamed macho. His height, his built, his gentleness, his voice, *and the way those pants fit nicely on him. Help me, Lord. All right, Joyce. Think on those things which are pure, lovely, exalting... well, he is lovely.* She leaned herself back against her couch, *Girl, you gotta do better.*

He returned with her water and sat it down in front of her. She grabbed it, thankful that he opened it for her, and took a long swig before allowing her gaze to fall on him. He sat next to her, grabbed her free hand, and began to massage it.

"Clint?" She placed the bottle back on the table top and withdrew her hands from his. "What's... going on? What is all this?"

"I don't know. All I know is... these past few months I've looked at you and saw another woman. I look at you and... see a woman I'm attracted to. A woman I want to be with."

"Why? Because I got saved and became available for you to date?" She asked the question, almost unsure if she wanted to hear the answer. She didn't know whether she would feel offended if all of a sudden he wanted her because she got saved. Is that the only thing that made her desirable? What about her beauty? Her intelligence? Her friendship?

"No. I don't know when it happened, but I woke up one morning and couldn't stop thinking about you. Then when I saw you, my heart melted and what I thought I felt for you as a friend flourished to something more. I was a little unsure of what was going on myself. Then I saw you that Sunday morning and you being next to me felt right... perfect."

Clint stopped speaking and waited for Joyce to intercept with feelings of her own. When a few minutes passed and she didn't say anything, Clint became even more nervous. *Maybe, I've been reading her wrong. What if she's not feeling what I'm feeling? Lord, I hope I did not tarnish this friendship.*

"Look, Joyce. I do cherish the friendship we have. You're a part of my life I don't ever want to live without. And if what I'm saying is freaking you out... then I'll step back. I have feelings for you, Joyce, but I would rather keep our friendship than to allow it to die because of this awkwardness."

Joyce wasn't sure what to think. What if they decided to pursue a relationship and it didn't work? Would their friendship come to an end? What if months down the line she falls deeply in love with him and he realizes she was just a rebound?

"You sure I'm not a rebound for Eileen?" Joyce asked.

"Rebound? Honey, no. Eileen and I were over before we ended it. And when we did, it was a mutual thing between the two of us, and we ended it on good terms," Clint responded.

"What if months from now you realize you've made a mistake? What happens to our friendship? We can't just go back if this relationship you want to try fails."

Clint grasped her hand again. "What if we fall in love and get married and have beautiful children? What if taking this friendship to the next level is the best thing we could have done? What if we're destined to be together, but because of fear we allow ourselves to be stuck here?"

Joyce didn't think of it that way, which made plenty more questions run across her mind. She felt the fear run up and down her back, but felt there was nothing she could do about it. She was stuck in a place, having to make a tough decision and was starting to feel frustrated that Clint put her in this predicament.

"I like you, Joyce. Really like you, and not like the 'friend' thing we've had for years. I know it's weird and strange and confusing maybe, but… I want to be with you. What I feel for you doesn't feel wrong. I've prayed and prayed and prayed, and I feel good about this."

Clint searched Joyce's eyes. Almost like he found what he was looking for, he nodded his head and squeezed her hand before lifting himself from the couch. "I know this is all strange and I've kind of sprung this on you. Take some time to think about it, and I promise whatever you decide will not change how this friendship goes. That's a promise."

Joyce still couldn't open her mouth to respond. Clint kissed her on the cheek before walking out. She finally released the breath she was holding, and took another deep breath smelling the masculine scent he left behind. *Lord, I need to pray.*

chapter 21

JOYCE WAS NOW doing better on her feet. Faithfully visiting her physical therapist every week paid off after all. After a month of therapy, she was able to walk without the crutches, and now two months later she was walking as if the accident never happened. Sitting down, standing up, or doing anything to contract her stomach muscles didn't scare her anymore, and she stopped having nightmares about Mariano. During the month of therapy it was easy to avoid Clint, although he called a few times. She would speak with him for a few minutes, then made up some excuse of why she had to go. She still wasn't ready to address the change in their friendship. The second month, his phone calls started dwindling and she found herself missing him.

She sat in her office, forcing herself to focus on catching up on projects. Although she had great employees who did an awesome job keeping the business running while she was out, she still had to sign final documents, make calls, and prepare contracts, and she couldn't do that with Clint bombarding her thoughts every five minutes.

She growled in frustration, throwing her pen across the room when she read the same document three times. *Why am I thinking about him so hard? God, help me.*

Ms. Ruby walked into Joyce's office, shutting the door behind her. "Here are the documents you've asked me for. Is there anything else you need?" She asked, placing the documents on the desk.

"No, Ms. Ruby. Thank you."

Instead of leaving, Ms. Ruby sat on the seat across from Joyce. Joyce glanced up and arched a brow. "Is there anything else, Ms. Ruby?"

"Yes, there is. Clint has called four times today. After you've told me the first two times you were unavailable, I came to the conclusion you didn't want to speak to him. Why not?"

"Ms. Ruby, I really don't think this—"

"Don't you dare use that high and mighty tone with me, young lady. I've been watching over you these last few years and you know I don't tolerate any disrespect. Now, that Clint has been a friend of yours since I've known you. Anytime he called, you answered. He came by, you dropped what you were doing. Anybody with a grain of sense in their head could tell you were crazy in love with that boy. What's happened?"

Joyce had known Ms. Ruby for years and knew she got relentless when she wanted to help. Trying to brush the situation off would not get her to leave. Plus, Joyce needed someone to talk to about how she was feeling. She closed the lid on her laptop and laid her head back against the headrest of her seat.

"Long story short... Clint told me two months ago he wanted more than just friendship. For years we've been friends, for years I've had the biggest crush on him, and now that I've gotten comfortable with just being friends he wants more."

"So, tell me what the problem is. What's keeping you?" Ms. Ruby questioned.

"I'm scared, Ms. Ruby. What if after a few months of dating he realize he'd made a mistake? Where will our friendship go from there?"

"Sweetheart, some of the best relationships begin with friendship. Every relationship needs a foundation, and what better foundation to start on than friendship. That just means you won't be blinded by love. Plus, friendship is where trust is built. Do you trust him?"

Without even thinking about it, Joyce answered, "Yes."

"And when you think about the perfect man to be married to, do you think of him?"

"I do."

"Then, Joyce, don't let fear keep you from being happy. Obviously, your heart always knew who you belonged to. It just took him some time to come aboard."

"So, you think I should pursue this?"

"No. Let him pursue, just allow yourself to be caught." Ms. Ruby answered, with a wide smile. "What you need to do is shut up fear, and listen to what your heart is saying. If I know you like I know you, then your heart has been saying Clint for years."

Joyce laughed as she sat up straight. She looked at Ms. Ruby and appreciated who she had become to her. Joyce thought about what she said and decided her happiness was worth more than listening to fear. Clint was a good man who wanted to give her what she'd been wanting for years... a great relationship with a great guy.

Ms. Ruby left her office and Joyce found herself dialing Clint's number.

"Hello?" Clint's deep, baritone voice came through the line.

Ignoring the tingling in her ear and the ball of nervous butterflies in her stomach Clint's voice always brought on, Joyce turned her seat around to gaze out her window. "Hey."

It took Clint a few seconds to respond, leaving Joyce a little nervous. "Hey yourself."

"Are you busy?" she asked.

"Not really. Just wrapping up some things before I leave for lunch. How are you?"

"I'm good. Trying to catch up on some things at the office. Kinda been busy."

"I kind of figured that after the fourth call."

Straight to it, huh. "Yeah. About that. I—"

"Look, Joyce. I understand I put you in a tough spot, and that was unfair of me. I shouldn't have assumed because my feelings for you changed, yours did for me. I've had some time to think about it, and I realized I've put you in an awkward position. I'm really sorry about that. I really value you as a friend, as a person, and I would hate for our friendship to end because of… because of a wrong move I made. I'm really hoping we could get pass this and remain friends." In a desperate tone, he added, "I don't want to lose you."

Joyce felt the wind knocked out of her as if she was sucker punched, and if she would have eaten breakfast that would have been next to follow. Her heart felt like it was being twisted into knots, and her vision blurred. She blinked and didn't feel the tear rolling down her face until it reached the side of her lip. She couldn't believe she missed her opportunity to be with the man she had always loved. For years she'd kept her feelings under wraps, and when he finally felt the way she did, she kept him waiting… and obviously waiting too long. *Gosh, I'm such an idiot.*

She couldn't even explain to herself why she kept him waiting, other than the fear that he changed his mind. She was too afraid that he came to his senses, and she wanted to beat him to the punch of ending something that never started.

"Clint, I…" Joyce felt her heart crack just a little bit more, and she knew within seconds she would be in tears. She had to get him off the line before he heard her breakdown. Clearing her throat, she tried a final time. "Clint, I have to go."

She hung up before he could say anything, and before he could hear her pitiful sob. She placed her head on her desk and allowed the tears to flow. Again, she allowed herself to be open and again she was disappointed. *Why can't I be happy, Lord? What am I doing wrong?*

She cried a few more minutes, then wiped her face, replenished her makeup and resolved that she would continue to do what she's done for years… bury her feelings inside and love her friend from afar.

❋ ❋ ❋

I'neta and Joseph were at the mall, window shopping for nothing in particular. Instead of having a picnic at the beach or taking a bike ride in the park like they usually do every Saturday, they decided to take a walk in the mall. It had been eight months since they've become a couple, and the camaraderie between them was priceless. The way Joseph cherished her opinions and how she felt, made her feel loved; and the way I'neta listened and respected what he had to say, made him love her even more. I'neta knew Joseph was set on marrying her, and she knew when the time came she wouldn't hesitate to say yes.

They stopped in front of a kiosk, and she watched him admire a sterling silver watch. His tall frame blocked her from seeing the crowd, but it didn't matter because she only had eyes for him. She smiled as she thought about how he smoothly slid his way into her life, broke down all her defenses, and built her trust. She didn't remember when it happened, but she looked at him one day and realized she was in love with this man. She trusted him with her life and knew that was one of the best choices she could have ever made.

They continued to walk around and she ran into a former classmate she wanted to stop and chat with for a while. Joseph whispered in her ear that he was going to walk around some more, but for her to take her time. Twenty minutes passed before he returned insisting that he needed to show her something.

He took her by the hand and led her into a jewelry store. A man stood behind a large glass case of earrings, smiled at her and handed Joseph something small in his hands. She expected he found a pair of diamond earrings similar to what she'd been admiring in a catalog for a few months now. *How sweet, he remembered.*

"Hey, I was wondering what you thought about this." Joseph took her hand and slid a two karat emerald cut diamond ring on her ring finger. All she remembered was something hitting her gut and her knees buckling from underneath her. By the time Joseph realized what was happening, I'neta had already hit the floor.

He picked her up and led her to a bench right outside the jewelry store, sat her down and fanned her with his hand. "Are you okay?" He asked once she seemed like she was coming to. He sat beside her and watched her with concern. He hoped he didn't scare her off. He knew she was comfortable with him, and the way she'd been smiling at him, holding his hands, and gazing into his eyes, he figured her feelings must have matured. *Was I wrong, Lord?*

No.

"What... I mean... I'm speechless. I really don't know what to say." I'neta stared at the ring like it was a spider stuck on her hand. She even tried to shake it off, but it wouldn't budge.

"Well, do I need to give you a hint?" Joseph asked her nervously. "I'neta, I know this comes as a shock, but I never held back how I feel for you since I fell in love with you. You are everything I desire in a wife. You're strong, loyal, open, forgiving, and I can go on and on but the list will never stop. You are my favor; you are my best friend. You are that piece that holds my heart together. Marrying you will be saying yes to my destiny, I'neta. Without you, my love, I have no future, because you are my future. I promise to protect you and love you as Christ does me. I promise to give you every desire of your heart, as long as you give me mine. And that, my love, would be you. Give me you and I will give you everything you so desire." He knelt down on his knees and squeezed her hand. "So, what do you say? Would you, I'neta Marie Villanucci, be my wife until death do us part?"

She stared at him in disbelief. The only sign she gave that showed anything he said touched her was a solitary tear gliding down her face, which he gently wiped off with his thumb. She knew with her heart what she should say, but her mouth wouldn't form the words.

I don't know if I'm ready. What if... what if I can't be strong for him? What if I'm not all that he sees? She closed her eyes, shut the voice in her head and assessed how she really felt. *I love this man. He's good to me. He doesn't pressure me to do anything I don't want to. He respects me.* She looked him in the eye as he silently and patiently awaited her answer. *And he loves me. Why can't I marry him?* A smile slowly lit her face, and she gave Joseph the answer he was praying for. "Yes, Joseph. I will marry you."

He scooped her up as if she weighed no more than sixty pounds and spun her around. The noise of the small crowd that gathered and watched unashamed could have reached the other side of the mall. He kissed her one last time before putting her down.

Wow! I'm going to be Mrs. Joseph Bernard Mills. She felt that punch in her gut again and fainted once more. This time, Joseph held her close and tight, and there was no way she was leaving his side.

***

After the phone call with Clint, Joyce tried to focus on work but it failed. She finally gave up and decided to take herself home and try again tomorrow. Lying on her couch, she found herself daydreaming about him, so to distract herself she decided to check her email. She deleted a few junk mails, responded to a forward from her cousin, and sent her mother an update about her health. She started to log off when she ran across an email that caught her attention. She clicked on it and froze. Afraid to continue on, she got up and walked away from her laptop, not sure if she should even read what it had to say.

It had been a little over three years since she had felt that familiar tug of fear for Noel, and this time she wasn't allowing it to cripple her. She made herself sit down in front of her laptop and read what he had to say.

Hey, Joyce.

How are you? I'm sure you've heard by now, I will be leaving this place and headed back home to Miami in a few days. I have written you hundreds of letters, but understand why you haven't written me back. I'm hoping since this was your email while we were together, you're still checking it. I thought about writing you another letter, but figure you probably trash them without opening them, so email was my next choice. Shoot, I don't even know if your home address is correct since I looked you up on line.

Again, I want to say how sorry I am about what I've done to you so many years ago. I was a selfish, angry, controlling, insecure man and I took that out on you. You did not deserve any of those things I've done, and I'm really sorry. I was hoping once I got out, you and I could meet for coffee somewhere so I can say this in person. I'm sure you don't want anything to do with me, and I promise I won't try to come on to you or anything like that. I just really need to see you and tell you this to your face

I know you're wondering why that is important. Well... I've been getting some counseling here and got into this substance abuse recovery group. One of our steps is apologizing to those we've hurt in our past. In order for me to move on, I've got to do this. I'll be staying with my cousin, Travis, when I get back home. I hope you see how sincere I am about clearing up our past, and get back with me soon.

See ya,
Noel

Joyce read it a few more times before shutting off her laptop and grabbing her purse to go out. She needed someone to talk to, and there was only one person she could think of. She drove contemplating whether this was a good move to make. At this time she was unsure about a lot of things. She was unsure about her friendship with Clint, she was unsure of how to respond to Noel, she was unsure of herself.

Usually, driving in Miami traffic made her angry and frustrated, but this time she used the time to rethink what she was doing. Tired of always allowing doubt to keep her from doing what she really wanted to do, she ignored the desperate tug to turn around.

Although, she purposed in her mind to ignore fear, she sat in her car for twenty minutes once she reached her destination. With her forehead resting on the steering wheel and her hands shaking uncontrollably, her mind came up with many reasons why she should start her car and turn back around. She almost did exactly that when she heard a soft tap on her passenger side window.

Looking up, she was greeted with a nervous smile from the man she never wanted to live without. She unlocked the door for him, and he slid his frame into the seat, shutting the door.

Knowing her so perfectly well, he didn't ask one question but allowed them to sit in silence for a few minutes. After noticing the shaking of her hand subsiding and the worried wrinkle leaving her face, he started the conversation.

"I was just getting back from lunch, and almost missed your car until I turned to look behind me and saw you sitting here. You okay?" He asked, tenderly.

She leaned her head against the head rest, hands still gripping the steering wheel, and eyes focused ahead. "No. I got an email from Noel today."

"OK. Seeing that he's been writing you for years, something must have been different about this one to make you this upset." Clint observed.

"I haven't told anyone but I'neta... he has been granted parole and should be out in a few days." She turned to look at Clint and saw mixed emotions run across his face.

"Seriously? How long have you knew?" He asked.

"A few months now. The judge wrote me a few months back letting me know he has been granted parole, and will be relocating to Miami. I just... I figured if I ignored it then something would change," she leaned her head back and stared at the beige ceiling of her car. "Gosh, Clint. I don't know what to do. He wants to meet to apologize about what he had done, and I feel like I need to at least give him that chance. I—"

Cutting her off, Clint angrily said, "You don't owe that man a thing, Joyce. What he did to you was ugly and mean. You broke it off, so let it stay broken. Gosh... don't be dumb about this."

For the first time since they've been friends, Joyce heard Clint raise his voice. And for the first time since they've been friends, Joyce felt offended by what he said. She knew he felt she was naïve about certain things, and she allowed people to take advantage of her... *But dumb?* She looked at him and saw the rage in his eyes, and wondered whether it was for her or because of her.

"You know. After I read the email, I had so many questions and feelings running through my mind. I needed someone to talk to, and the first person I thought about was you. Why? Because I trust you and value your opinion. I knew if anyone could help me get my thoughts together that person would be you. But never in a million years would I have thought you think I was dumb." So much hurt was laced in her words.

Clint immediately felt sorry about his word of choice. "I'm not calling you dumb. I don't think you're dumb. All I want you to do is think about what this man has done to you, and what he is now asking from you."

"I, more than anyone in my life, know what this man has done to me," she turned her body to give him her full attention, pleading with her eyes for him to understand. "Clint, I need to get pass what this man has done to me in order to live free from him. In order for me to get pass this, I need to forgive him, and forgiveness can be a tricky thing when a person is thousands of miles away. I know in my mind I have forgiven him, but I need to know in my heart. I truly believe I need to see him in order to be sure that I have forgiven him entirely. Can you understand that?"

Clint not only saw the pleading in her eyes, but heard it in her voice. He struggled with wanting to protect her from ever being hurt again, and staying in his lane as a friend. He couldn't help but wonder whether she still harbored feelings for her ex, turning him down in return.

"Is this why you didn't want to take things further with us?" Clint asked.

"This has nothing to do with us. I don't have feelings for Noel, Clint. This has nothing to do with reconciling our relationship or seeing where we can go from here. I know what kind of man he is... or was, and that's a part of my life I don't want to relive. But I need to forgive this man, or at least know for sure whether I have." She reached over to grab his hand. "He's no longer a part of my life, and I want to make sure his ghost doesn't linger on."

Clint understood what she meant, and had to come to terms that things between them could not be resolve until she cleared up her past. Without her totally forgiving Noel, she would never trust another man wholeheartedly, and being in a relationship where fear has an opportunity to show its ugly head was not what Clint wanted. He nodded his understanding, gave her one last look, and climbed out of her car.

chapter 22

JOYCE SAT AT the local Cuban coffee shop in downtown Miami, surrounded by other patrons having loud colorful conversations. She sat facing the entrance as she sipped on a small cup of Cuban coffee and nipped on a guava pastry. Three times already she grabbed her purse to leave, but knew she couldn't allow fear to keep her from doing this. It had been a week since she'd responded to Noel's email and they agreed to meet here for coffee. Her nervousness made her arrive thirty minutes early, and watched the door for his arrival.

Five minutes late, she watched Noel stand outside the door and remove his hat before coming in. She watched him look around the room and saw recognition flash in his eyes when he saw her. His brisk smile reminded her of why she first was attracted to him years ago.

Sitting on a bench to catch a breather one Saturday afternoon while shopping at one of the largest malls in Miami, she took a swig from her water bottle and almost choked when she caught a handsome, average weight, chocolate complexion guy staring at her. He stood a little below six feet, dressed in casual jeans and designer T-shirt. Their eyes locked and he gave a brisk smile before making his way to her. She watched him walk towards her, and smiled when he sat next to her. They talked about the city, shopping, movies before he finally asked her name and number. They talked on the phone every night for two weeks before she agreed to go to dinner with him.

She remembered sitting at parades holding hands, kissing at the movies, dancing at a concert, and staring into each other eyes at dinners for months before he said he loved her. They dated for a year before she moved in with him, and that's when things started to go sour. He wanted her to stay home more while he went out. He complained about her friends coming over, and always made a fuss about dinner not being ready. The first time he hit her was after six months of living together. She had made plans to go out with a few of her friends, and he wanted her to stay home. In the middle of them arguing he punched her in the eye, then said 'Let's see if you can go out with a black eye.' He walked out and she canceled plans with her friends, wondering how she got into this mess.

Noel came home hours later, took a shower, laid next to her in bed as she played like she was asleep, and wrapped his arm around her. The next morning she woke up with breakfast already made and him apologizing for hitting her. That was the first apology of many to follow for years after that.

As she watched him approach her now, she wondered why it took her so long to leave him. He took the seat across from her and looked at her for a while before speaking.

"You look good, Joyce," Noel said.

"Thank you. You look the same," she responded.

"I was surprised you were willing to see me today. I really didn't expect to get a response from you."

"Well... we were years ago and I've changed, Noel."

"I see that. So... how have you been?" He asked.

"Good. Look... I really don't have the time for small talk. I have to head back to my office soon." She said in order to keep the meeting where it's supposed to be. *No remember when, what could have been... No. Apologize and cease all contact here.*

"OK. I hear you. I guess I'll get right to the point," he said, clearing his throat and briefly avoiding eye contact. "When we first met, I was head over heels in love with you. You were gorgeous, smart, independent. You laughed at all my jokes and looked at me with so much admiration in your eyes," the smile on his face evidence of the history he remembered.

"Then we moved in together. I got fired, was in between jobs, and started to feel a little disgusted with myself. Here I am, I've asked my girl to move in with me just when I thought I was in the prime of my life, and BAM, I lose my job. I didn't know how to face you knowing I was supposed to be the provider. After months of putting in resumes, going to interviews, working temp jobs I felt inadequate. After a while, I thought you felt the same way about me, and the anger, disgust, and disappointment I felt took over."

He risked a look at Joyce, and continued when he didn't see the hatred he was expecting. "I felt I didn't have any control over anything. You were basically taking care of us... paying the bills, buying groceries, clothes. Then it seemed like you were going out every other night, not wanting to spend time with me, and I got afraid I was losing you," he rubbed his eyes before releasing a deep breath.

"The first time I hit you, I was really sorry about it. But it seemed to get easier to do each time, and the fear I saw made me feel good for once. As crazy and foolish as that sounds, I'm ashamed to say it's the truth. I was a coward who underestimated you, and took advantage of the strength I had over you," he said, looking Joyce in the eyes. "The night I... I threw you down the stairs, I don't know what I was thinking. And I know I would never understand what you had to feel over the passing of our child."

Taking another deep breath, Noel continued, "Our unborn child is what made me change while I was in prison," shaking his head, he stared at his hands. "If you would have told me days before that night I would have ended up in prison for that, I would have bet my life on it. I would have never thought..." clearing his throat, he looked at Joyce again. "I am really sorry, Joyce. For everything. The way that we ended up was never how I imagined us to be. I know it's been years, but I could only hope that you would forgive me."

He sat back on his seat and exhaled as if he had been holding that in for years. She watched his movements, his facial expression, his demeanor the entire time and knew in her heart he was sincere. She sat back in amazement… not at how he changed, but at how she felt. She didn't feel the fear she once felt around him, she didn't feel angry, and she didn't feel attraction. She looked at him and felt sorry. Sorry that his insecurities led him into prison and her childless.

She folded her hands and looked Noel directly in the eyes, something she wasn't able to do years ago. "It was very unfortunate how things ended between us, and I doubt you would ever know what I felt when I lost our child. But please understand this. For more my sake than yours, I forgive you, Noel. In order for me to be totally free of you, I have to let you go." She smiled and knew what she said was true. "You know… I truly believe without forgiving you I would never be able to love anyone completely, or trust them the way they deserve to be trusted. And I deserve to be in a relationship where love and trust is not questioned. I deserve to be with a man who would love me with no reservations. I forgive you, Noel, because forgiving you allows true love to find me and allows me to accept it."

"And you do deserve all of that," Noel responded. "Thank you, Joyce. Really. And… whoever the guy is… he's a lucky man."

Joyce smiled, grabbed her purse, and stood to leave. "And I'm a lucky woman." She walked off leaving Noel, her past, her half finished coffee and guava pastry behind.

✳ ✳ ✳

Clint sat in his office discussing with two interns what he needed done for a particular project they were currently working on. He found himself distracted, looking at the clock numerous of times, wondering how Joyce's meeting with her ex was going. After the fourth time of having to explain himself, confusing both interns, one of them finally made a suggestion.

"Mr. McCord… how about you allow me and James to take a ten minute break, just to get some fresh air?"

Clint knew the guys wanted to take a smoke break, and as much as he didn't agree with it he needed a break also. He nodded his head to excuse them, and went to pour himself a cup of coffee from the lobby. As he sipped and walked back into his office, he struggled with the idea of calling Joyce. He stood in front of his window wondering how the conversation was going. *Would she realize she still have feelings for Noel and agree to continue where they ended? That would be a terrible idea. Would Noel be the same guy he was years ago and force her to do something she didn't want to do? I'll kill him.*

Clint didn't realize he stood at his window for ten minutes until James and Roger walked back in. "Are you ready, Boss?" Roger asked.

"How about we call it a day, gentlemen? Let's come back tomorrow and smooth out the details," Clint said.

"Well," Roger looked at James and answered for both of them. "That sounds good to us if that's what you want to do, Boss."

"Yeah," Clint walked back to his desk, dismissing them with a nod. "You guys can leave. I expect to see you first thing in the morning."

"Eight o'clock sharp, Sir," James responded. "Thank you." They both scurried out before Clint could change his mind. He sat on his seat, leaned his head back, and gently rotated the chair in circles. Staring at the ceiling, he prayed Joyce made the right decision.

"Wow. You look as productive as a cat watching paint dry. Is this what you get paid to do?" Joyce asked while leaning against his office door.

Clint stopped the chair and looked at her, hoping to read her expression. He watched her every step as she walked towards him and sat on one of the vacant seats in front of his desk.

"I just saw your interns leave. They ran out like there was a fire to take out," she said.

"I just let them go for the day. Couldn't get much work done here."

"Yeah? Why not? Twirling around in circles ain't working for you?" she asked.

Clint leaned forward in his chair, elbows on his desk, and looked her directly in the eyes. "Worried about you."

Joyce looked away, still unsure on how to handle what she kept reading in Clint's eyes. If she wasn't mistaken she would have sworn she saw love, hope, and attraction flicker in his eyes.

"Now, why would you be worried about me?"

Instead of answering her question, Clint asked one of his own. "How did your meeting go with Noel?"

"Well... he talked a little about our past and the way that he felt. He said he was head over heels in love with me, thought I was beautiful, smart, independent. Said he was at the prime of his life when he asked me to move in with him."

Clint leaned back on his seat, not liking where this was going.

Joyce saw his expression and continued on. "He said when he lost his job and had to rely on me, he felt disgusted and ashamed of himself, thought he was going to lose me and that's when the beatings started. He even mentioned our child and..." swallowing the lump in her throat, she paused for a second. "Anyways... he apologized for what he did, and... and I truly believe he was sincere, Clint."

Clint's heart dropped and he knew then Joyce went back to Noel. The way she talked about it, the way her eyes gleamed, and the fact that she believed him was all the evidence he needed. Not being able to sit still and look at her while his heart breaks, he stood up and looked out his window, turning his back on her.

"So... what now?" He asked.

"Well... I told him I forgave him. Not for him, but more for me." She stood up and slowly made her way to Clint. "See... I told him in order for me to be free of him completely, I needed to forgive him. In order for true love to find me, I have to let him go. How else can I freely love and trust the man of my dreams if I allow what he did hang over my head? I deserve to be loved by a great man, and he deserves for me to love him in return. I deserve to be in a healthy relationship, I deserve to be with the man I've been in love with for the past seven years." She stopped just nearly inches away from behind him. "I mean... it took him long enough to realize all he ever needed was right under his nose, but I am so glad he waited as long as he did. I wasn't ready then, but I am ready now to show him I'm not afraid to be loved by him."

Joyce watched as her words sunk into Clint's head as his shoulders relaxed. He slowly turned to face her and stared at her for a while before responding. "So... you didn't go back to Noel?"

"Heavens, no. Why would I?" She took another step towards him, almost closing the gap between them. "Clint... I love you. I always have. It's just... I've gotten comfortable hiding it all these years, and then I got scared it may ruin our friendship. But I realize that our friendship is the best way for us to start this relationship. I trust you Clint, and there is no one else I would want to be with. I just hope you haven't really changed your mind about... wanting me."

Clint stared at her without saying a word. He watched doubt flicker in her eyes for a brief second, before seeing hope. He took the final step to close the small space between them, and gently cupped her face in his hands.

"You don't know how happy I am to hear you say those words. It drove me crazy all afternoon wondering what was going on between you two. I just couldn't bear the thought of losing you to him... and right after I've... just realized how much I care for you." Without any hesitation he pulled her into his arms, loving the feel of her there. "Joyce, I want you to be mine. My friend, my girl, and when the time is right... my wife."

Joyce wrapped her arms around his waist and hugged him in return. Loving how wonderful this felt, and how perfect she fit into his arms, she looked up at him and smiled. "I love the sound of that."

For years she imagined what it would be like to be held this way by him. In all her imagining she never thought it would be like this. She leaned her head against his chest, and thanked God for great moments like these. *Who would have thought forgiveness felt this good.*

Epilogue

JOYCE SAT IN the dressing room, patiently waiting for I'neta to come out in the fifth wedding dress she had tried on for the day. Surrounded by hundreds of white wedding gowns and mirrors, Joyce wondered how much longer this was going to take. For the past six months she had been running around Miami with I'neta looking at banquet halls, trying on dresses, and looking at cakes. It was all exciting and crazy, especially since I'neta still had another six months before her wedding day. Joyce was honored when I'neta asked her to be her maid of honor, but she really didn't expect to be running around like a chicken with its head cut off.

While Joyce was exhausted from all the crazy wedding plans, she secretly stored information in her mind for when her time came. She and Clint had been taking it slow for the last six months, but love was definitely in the air. She was afraid their friendship would change when they decided to become something more; however, things remained the same. They ran together in the mornings, still had lunch dates, and hung out. The only differences were they held hands more, found reasons to share soft touches, and Joyce got to steal little kisses from him when he wasn't expecting it. They made sure their time together didn't lead to more than they could handle, and surprisingly Joyce hadn't found herself compromising.

She found herself reading her Bible more and praying. Her desire to please God kept her from making mistakes, and she assumed it was the same way with Clint.

Clint was such an amazing and patient man. She thought about the conversation they had a few nights ago. They were watching a comedy show at her house, when Clint reached for her hand, kissed her forehead, and whispered softly in her ear, "I can see us doing this forever. Wedding bands on our fingers, a few kids running around, a huge house to put them all in."

He chuckled but Joyce found herself across the room and headed towards the kitchen. "I'm thirsty. Do you want something to drink?"

She didn't know how to respond, so she avoided the subject as best as she could. Clint let it go until after the show. He turned to her with worry in his eyes, "Do you... where are we headed in this relationship, Joyce? In your eyes, am I just someone to date or do we have a future together?"

Joyce hated the hurt look in his eyes. She laid her head on his chest and told him the truth. "I love you, Clint, and want more than ever to have this forever. The marriage, kids, big house... you. All of it. I... I'm just not ready for this conversation. I'm happy where we are."

"So, how long do you want to stay 'here'?" Clint asked confused.

"Until we're both ready for the next stage," she looked at him then. "I'm here, Clint, and there's no need to rush. Let me enjoy this with you."

He held her closer and sighed heavily. "I hear you, Love. I hear you. We'll take it as slow as we need to."

She giggled and wondered what 'slow' meant for Clint. She knew he'd bring the topic up again soon. Leaning against the soft cushioned bench in the dressing room, Joyce felt great that such a good man wanted to spend the rest of his life with her.

"What got you smiling so hard? It better be this dress I have on," I'neta interrupted her thoughts.

Joyce sat up and admired the halter wedding dress I'neta gracefully wore. White pearls outlined the bodice and waist, and ran straight down the center of the back all the way to the train. I'neta twirled a few times before asking Joyce, "How does it look?"

"Gorgeous. But every dress you've tried on has been gorgeous. The question is... do you feel like it's the one?" Joyce responded.

I'neta looked at herself a few seconds longer before answering. "No. I mean, I love the halter and the bodice and how great it looks on me... but I don't feel that special umph about it. You know what I mean?" She turned to seek Joyce's understanding.

"Well... I've never shopped for a wedding dress before, but I do know what you mean. It's almost like knowing when the guy is 'the one'."

"Yes. Exactly like that... almost." I'neta twirled a few more times before stepping off the pedal stool and headed to the changing room. When she returned, she had on a yellow sundress and hot pink sandals.

"Let's go get something to eat. I'm hungry." I'neta grabbed her hot pink handbag from Joyce and walked out the store. Joyce thanked the attendant before following her out.

They stopped at a small bakery not too far from where they were, and I'neta ordered a turkey sandwich on a croissant, while Joyce ordered a tuna sandwich on rye bread. They sat outside and people watched, while eating their sandwiches in companionable silence.

Joyce finished her sandwich and drank half of her tea before breaking the silence. "So, still no update on Mason?"

I'neta sighed. "No. But you know what? I'm not one bit worried about it. He's probably up north somewhere. He hasn't made any attempt to contact me, so as far as I'm concerned he's history." Leaning back against her seat, she shrugged. "I'm really good. Everything in my life right now is good."

Joyce gave I'neta her full attention, and smiled. "It's good to see you so happy and... content." Joyce said.

I'neta's face lit up in a smile. "That's exactly what I am... content. I have never felt so comfortable with a man, ever in my life. Well, besides my father you know." Her eyes gleamed with tears. "I feel so blessed right now. I have a man who genuinely loves me; my father will be released from jail soon and moving here, and best of all... I am more in love with God than I've ever been in my life. Doesn't it seem like once we gave Him our full heart everything else lined up?" I'neta asked in amazement.

"Our lives got better, our men found us, our hearts got healed." Joyce answered in the same amazement. "We forgave, and it brought us love."

"And all because we told God 'yes'. Who wouldn't want to serve a God like this!" I'neta laughed and drunk the last of her lemonade. She looked at her watch and grabbed her handbag. "I have to meet Joseph in about an hour. We have a meeting with the caterer, and then marriage counseling." I'neta stood and leaned down to give Joyce a kiss on the cheek. "I love you, Friend. And I hear wedding bells ringing in the future for you, too."

Joyce laughed and hugged her friend's neck. "I love you, too, Chick."

Watching her friend walk away, Joyce sipped on her tea then softly whispered, "I hear them, too, and its sweet music to my ears."

The End